THE BLACK HEART

SUSAN K. DRONEY

This is a work of fiction. Names, characters, places, and incidents are products of the author's imagination or are used fictitiously and are not to be construed as real. Any resemblance to actual events, locations, organizations, or persons, living or dead, is entirely coincidental.

World Castle Publishing, LLC
Pensacola, Florida
Copyright © Susan K. Droney 2017
Paperback ISBN: 9781629896977
eBook ISBN: 9781629896984
First Edition World Castle Publishing, LLC, May 22, 2017
http://www.worldcastlepublishing.com

Licensing Notes

Cover: Karen Fuller
Editor: Lisa Petrocelli

CHAPTER ONE

Carter Rogers sat at his kitchen table sipping a cup of coffee. He watched as a gentle breeze softly moved the curtains on the open window. It was an unusually warm evening for early May, but not warm enough to need air conditioning. He loved nights like this with the fresh air coming through the windows. He breathed deeply and then pushed back his chair and stood. He was setting his coffee cup in the dishwasher when an explosion sounded in the distance. The force was strong enough to rattle the dishes in the cupboard. Almost immediately, sirens could be heard in the distance.

Carter turned to his wife Morgan who was wiping down the counter. "I wonder what that was."

"Probably just some kids setting off firecrackers," Morgan replied with a slight shrug. She glanced at her wristwatch. It read exactly nine o'clock.

He shook his head. "I don't think so. Something's exploded," he said. "Don't you hear the sirens?"

She cocked an eyebrow. "I'm sure it's nothing serious." She smiled. "Would you like to watch TV or go to a movie? There's a new mystery I've been wanting to see. It doesn't start until ten. We could get a sitter," she said hopefully.

"Morgan, I'm too tired tonight. Besides, I doubt we'd find a sitter this late. Anyway, I don't like to do things on the spur of the moment. You know that."

She frowned. "I'm sorry. I just thought that maybe for once in your life you might want to do something spontaneous instead of mapping your life out minute by minute. Next time I'll ask you a month in advance so you can pencil it into your schedule."

Carter laughed at her sarcasm. "I'm sorry, honey." He came up behind her and put his arms around her slim waist. "We'll do something special tomorrow night. I promise. I already have it penciled in."

Morgan turned around facing him. "I suppose I'll let you off the hook. But no excuses tomorrow night. I'll line up a sitter."

"I'll even spring for dinner first. We'll make a night of it."

"I'm looking forward to it." She brushed his sandy brown hair from his brow. "Looks like you need a trim."

"I think I'll let it grow out a little."

Morgan began to reply, but the phone rang interrupting her.

"I'll get it," Carter said.

Morgan finished straightening the kitchen, tuning out her husband's phone conversation. She had other things on her mind to mull over. She jumped when Carter placed a heavy hand on her shoulder. "What's the matter, Carter?" He was ashen-faced and trembling.

He pulled her close and held her like he was afraid to

let go.

"Carter…what's happened?" she asked anxiously.

He drew a shuddering breath. "It's Mom," he choked. "Her house just blew up. That's the explosion we heard. Hunter said she'd been to his house for dinner and he'd taken her home only a little while before." He shook his head in disbelief. "Hunter left only half an hour ago. He said he walked her inside and didn't notice anything unusual. There was no gas smell or anything." Carter blinked hard. "I've got to get over there," he said hoarsely. "But first I'm going over to Hunter's house."

"Don't go right now, honey," Morgan said gently. "There's nothing you can do."

He looked into her eyes. "My mother has just been killed. I want to be there." Tears brimmed in his eyes. "I need some answers." He took his jacket from the coatrack.

Morgan hugged him. "I'm so sorry, Carter," she whispered. She suppressed the smile tugging at the corners of her mouth. "I'll wait up for you."

He nodded and walked out of the house.

Morgan watched him leave, and then walked upstairs and into her daughter's bedroom. She gently caressed her sleeping child's cheek and tucked a blanket around her. Yesterday Becca celebrated her first birthday. Morgan smiled as she bent and kissed Becca. "I love you, baby. Have pleasant dreams," she said softly.

****

Carter, racing to Hunter's house on the north side of town, ran both red lights and signs. He was glad there were no cops around to delay him. They were all most likely at his mother's house anyway. He pulled into the driveway and cut the engine, then hurried out of the car and up the walk to the front door where Hunter's wife Emily waited for him. Tears streamed down her round face.

"Mom's dead, Carter," she cried, throwing herself into his arms. "Oh my God. I can't believe Mom's dead."

"I know," he said hoarsely. He stood unsteadily as he tried to support himself and Emily. He was still trying to come to terms with the fact that his mother was dead. He became nauseous. He felt like he was standing outside of his body watching it go through the motions. He swallowed the bile rising in his throat. "Where's Hunter?" His voice sounded unnatural.

Emily moved away from him running a hand through her short brown hair. She nodded toward the door. "In there." She sniffed. "I...I sent the kids to a neighbor's for the night. I don't know what to tell Justin and Beth."

"Don't worry about that right now," Carter said in a low voice.

She wiped her eyes with a damp tissue. "I don't know what to do for Hunter, Carter. He's fallen apart. He blames himself."

He squeezed her shoulder. "I'll talk to him." He took a deep breath, and then grabbed the doorknob to balance himself. After a few seconds, he entered the house. Hunter sat on the sofa with his head between his large hands. His hair was rumpled. Carter walked over to his older brother and sat next to him, putting an arm around Hunter's husky shoulders.

Hunter raised his head. Tears were splashed on his

face. "How could something like this happen, Carter?" he moaned. "She was just here—" He threw his hands in the air. "In this house for dinner." He shook his head.

Carter frowned. "You said you drove her home. She didn't drive over?"

"Her car's in the garage."

"What's wrong with her car?"

"I don't know. She said something about the brakes. She drove it to the garage and I picked her up there and brought her here for dinner."

"Do you know if she went to work today?"

He nodded. "Yeah."

"Did she stop home before driving to the garage?" Carter asked.

"I don't know, Carter. What's with all the questions?" Hunter clasped his hands together.

"Sorry. I'm just trying to make some sense out of this." Carter rose. He shoved his hands into his pants pockets and stood with his back to his brother staring into space.

"Nothing about it makes any sense," his brother replied. "I was supposed to give her a ride to work in the morning and then Emily was going to pick her up later. She didn't know how long her car would be in the garage." His voice broke. "Why did this happen, Carter?"

"I don't know, Hunter. Maybe there was a gas leak. Was the gas company doing any work in the area?"

"Not that I'm aware of. And I would have smelled gas. And you know Mom's keen sense of smell. She would have known right away. I walked her inside and everything was fine."

Carter turned around and faced his brother. "I'm going over to Mom's house. I need to see the extent of the damage. Maybe get some answers."

"I doubt there's anything left to see from what Jake Birch said when he called. He was going to call you, but I told him I would."

He shrugged. "Well, maybe Jake has some news." He sighed. "Do you want to come with me?"

"No." He shook his head. "I...I can't." He swallowed hard. "I don't want to see it. I don't think I'll ever drive near that part of town again."

"I understand," Carter said quietly. "I'll be back later." Still numb, he walked outside. He wished he'd wake up in his bed cuddled next to Morgan and find out it was only a bad dream. He sucked a large amount of air into his lungs as he glanced around Hunter's house. He had designed the house two years ago. It was a beautiful four-bedroom two-story home with high ceilings, a formal living and dining room, large family room, kitchen with two islands and a large eating area, and a bright sunroom at the end of the house.

He walked to the back of the house and seated himself on a picnic bench. He looked out into the expansive backyard. His mind wandered as he thought of happier times and then not so happy times. Bits and pieces of thoughts and conversations randomly filtered through his mind. He'd always been tight with his family and had been sorely disappointed when they hadn't accepted his young wife into the family as they had his brothers' wives. They were polite enough but never made much of an effort to make her feel a part of them. He had hoped they'd welcome her with open arms, but they'd remained aloof. Morgan had confided in him that she was hurt because of their cool reception toward her.

Consequently, he didn't spend as much time with his family as he had before he'd met Morgan. He missed them. Every weekend in the summer one of them had a barbeque. And every Sunday since he could remember, dinner was at his mother's. But that changed, too. Morgan refused to go and insisted that since Carter was married, he should stay home and allow her to cook dinner for them. She did invite his family over occasionally, mostly at his urging, but the tension was so thick that it made him walk on eggshells and he was relieved when they'd leave. Eventually his family refused further invitations. That put Carter smack in the middle. He did his best to keep peace, but nonetheless, he was deeply disturbed that his family and wife would never get along.

He'd come right out and asked his mother what it was about Morgan that prevented her and his siblings from accepting Morgan into the family. She hadn't minced words with him. According to her, Morgan had two sides to her personality, the kind, loving and compassionate side she showed to him, but the manipulative, hateful side she showed to others outside of his presence. He'd scoffed and told his mother he didn't believe that and beseeched her to give Morgan a chance and to ask the other family members to do the same. Things hadn't changed between his family and his wife, so he resigned himself to the fact they never would. He loved his family, but was crushed that they wanted little or nothing to do with his wife. They were putting him in an impossible situation and forcing him to make a choice he didn't want to make. But he knew if it eventually came down to it, he would choose his wife. She'd captured his heart from the first moment he'd set eyes on her.

He thought the birth of his daughter would bring everyone together, but it only seemed to make matters worse. His mother worshipped Becca, but Morgan rarely let her see her granddaughter. It broke her heart. Carter took Becca for visits as often as he could, but Morgan refused to let Becca spend the night and wouldn't allow her grandmother to babysit. He'd tried to talk to Morgan about how it wasn't fair to use Becca, but Morgan would accuse him of siding with his family against her. She'd even threatened to take Becca and leave if that would make life easier for him. She told him that deep down maybe that was what he wanted. It wasn't. He couldn't bear being away from her or his daughter. Carter still had held on to the hope that in time they'd become as close as his brothers' wives were to his mother, but now that would never happen. He closed his eyes for a moment, and then pulled himself to his feet. He walked back around to the front of the house and stood for a few minutes, and then got into his car.

Twenty minutes later, he arrived at the familiar neighborhood. It was swarming with residents from the surrounding neighborhoods and curious onlookers. He told the officer blocking the street who he was and was granted access. The street was filled with police cars, fire trucks, and other vehicles. He wasn't prepared for the sight that awaited him. He squinted, thinking his eyes were playing tricks on him as he stared in disbelief at the pile of rubble that had once been his boyhood home. Tears stung his eyes and he broke out in a cold sweat.

Sheriff Jake Birch walked over to him. "I'm sorry, Carter."

Carter threw his hands up. "What the hell happened, Jake? Does anyone know?" His eyes searched the older man's face for some sort of explanation.

Jake slowly shook his head. "We don't know anything for certain yet, Carter. It might take some time to find out what exactly happened."

"You must know something!" Carter demanded. "What about my mother?"

Jake's eyes swept over the smoldering debris. "Carter, you can see for yourself…she didn't have a chance. I'm sorry," he said sympathetically.

"The investigators must have some idea of what happened here. A house just doesn't explode! Was it a gas leak? Hunter said there was no smell of gas when he walked her inside the house."

Jake looked uncomfortably at the ground for a few seconds before raising his eyes to meet Carter's. "It wasn't an accident or a gas explosion. You have a right to know that."

Carter froze. "What?" His body shook. "Are you saying what I think you are?" He choked. "She was murdered?"

He thoughtfully scratched his chin. "We've never had anything like this happen around these parts, Carter. You know that." He looked evenly at him. "We need to determine the motive."

Carter emphatically shook his head. "What vendetta could anyone possibly have against my mother? It doesn't make sense! Who would want her dead?" His eyes narrowed. "My mother didn't have any enemies. You know that, Jake.

Could it be a random act?"

"I don't know, Carter."

Carter's nostrils filled with the stench of the smoldering ruins. He coughed, and then spat at the ground. "Fill me in on what you do know, Jake."

"There's not too much at this point," he answered, pulling on his chin.

"I've known you my entire life, Jake. You must have a theory."

Jake was thoughtful for a moment. "I do."

"And?" Carter persisted.

His eyes slanted. "My theory is that the perpetrator knew your mother would be out this evening. He then entered the house and rigged up a device in her bedroom lamp that would detonate the moment she turned the lamp on." He paused. "After the lamp was turned on, everything just blew."

Carter grabbed the sheriff's arm. "A bomb? Why? What could my mother have ever done to cause someone to want to blow up her house with her in it? It still doesn't make sense."

"Remember, Carter, it's only my theory. I didn't say it was fact."

"It's quite an elaborate theory, Jake." Carter eyed him warily.

"But it is still only my theory. I'd wait until the cause officially comes out before you say anything."

Carter turned when a reporter stuck a microphone in his face.

"We'd like to ask you a few questions, Mr. Rogers," the young reporter said as he instructed his cameraman where to stand.

"Not now," Carter said.

"How did you feel when you heard your mother's house had exploded?"

Carter pushed the microphone away from his face.

"There's speculation that a bomb was planted in her house. Do you know anything about that?"

Jake stepped in front of the reporter. "We have no comment at this time. A report will be issued after the initial investigation is completed. You need to clear this area immediately." He signaled to a deputy. "Get the media out of here now!"

"I'm sorry about that," Jake apologized after the reporter had left. "I suppose you'll be hounded for a while. I'll do my best to keep them away from you and your family."

"Thank you, Jake. I appreciate that." He ran a hand threw his hair. "I still feel like this is a bad dream and I'll wake up at any moment." He swallowed hard as his eyes swept the area. "I can't imagine what went through her mind."

"I don't think your mother felt anything, Carter. It happened too quickly."

Carter cleared his throat. "I need to believe that, Jake. If I knew she suffered in any way…" His voice trailed off.

"I know."

Carter was silent as he panned the smoking debris. "What did she do to deserve this?"

"We'll do everything in our power to find the answers."

"I know you will, Jake." His eyes narrowed. "Hunter called me right after you notified him."

"I called him because I passed your mother and him

when, I assume, he was giving her a lift to her house. He said he'd call you immediately."

"He did. He couldn't bring himself to come back here." Carter's forehead furrowed. "Mom had dinner at his house tonight. Her car is in the garage. That's why he was giving her a ride."

"Is Hunter going to notify the rest of the family?"

"He's not in any shape," Carter replied. "I suppose I'll have to do it."

"Look. I can do it if it'll help," Jake offered. "Your family has always been like my own."

"Thank you. The girls are going to fall apart," Carter said.

Jake hugged him. "If it's the last thing I do, I'll find out who did this."

CHAPTER TWO

Morgan quietly slipped out of Becca's room and into the master bedroom and flicked on the light. She focused on her movements in the full-length mirror on the opposite end of the wall and smiled as she gently moved her fingers down her sides, caressing herself. She was beautiful and she knew it. Her chestnut hair hung loosely over her slim shoulders. Her looks were the one thing no one had ever been able to take from her and which she had always been able to use to her advantage. Vanity was never one of her faults and she'd realized a long time ago that it was all right to be vain as long as one knew the truth about him or herself. She admired her youthful trim figure. It had been easy to return to her normal weight and tone up her body after the birth of her child. She wondered why so many women used childbirth as an excuse to let themselves get fat and out of shape. Just lazy, she thought. An excuse to lie around and complain.

Morgan hummed softly as she looked at the clock on the nightstand. It read 10:28 p.m. She picked up a framed photograph of Carter and held it tightly to her chest for a few seconds. She set the photo down, then squatted, and felt underneath the nightstand and pulled out a small metal box. She took a key from her jeans pocket and quickly unlocked the box and threw back the lid and surveyed the contents. A single piece of yellow lined paper from a legal pad lay on top. She picked up the paper and stared at it for a long minute. The name Rachel Rogers glared back at her. Morgan thought about Carter. Her heart ached for the pain his family inflicted on him. She could never stand to see him hurting, but his family continued hurting him every day and she would tolerate it no longer. They didn't care about his happiness the way she did. He needed her much more than he ever realized, but his family only wanted to tear them apart. She needed to stop that. The time had come. There was no other way. Someday he would understand. He loved her and would forgive her anything as long as it meant they could live in peace without the encumbrances of his family.

She grinned as she took a red pen from the box, and next to Rachel's name neatly printed: "Completed May 6, 1983."

****

Carter threw his car keys on the kitchen table, and then walked toward the living room. He stopped before entering the room. Morgan was engrossed in a horror movie on TV and didn't appear to hear or see him. He watched his young, beautiful wife for a few minutes. He was a lucky man and he knew any man would trade places with him in a minute. Life had mostly been good to him blessing him with a successful business, an adoring wife, and a precious child. He had what every man wanted, but so few seemed to acquire. Had he been so complacent in his life, aside from the discord between his wife and family, that he'd somehow thought he was immune

16

from tragedy? He'd never thought he'd lose his mother, or anyone close to him for that matter, in such a horrific way. He didn't know how to cope with the pain coursing through him. What he did know though was that he needed Morgan like he'd never needed her before. He wanted to lean on her and seize some of her strength or he'd never get through this.

"Jake Birch thinks Mom was murdered," he said in a barely audible voice. He didn't care that he'd promised Jake he wouldn't talk about his suspicions. He couldn't keep it to himself.

"Honey, no!" Morgan exclaimed, jumping to her feet and rushing to his side. She wrapped her arms around his waist and held him tightly for what seemed to him like minutes, but was in reality only seconds. He savored the closeness of her, taking in the light fragrance she wore, the familiarity. This was normal. God, how he needed everything to be back to normal. Morgan made him feel like everything would be all right again.

She released him and looked into his eyes. "Let me fix you a drink."

"No." He shook his head. "I don't want a drink."

She studied him. "Have you contacted the rest of the family?"

"Jake's going to do it. I can't deal with it right now." He walked to the sofa and sat down. "I'll have to make the funeral arrangements, though. Hunter's not in any condition to do it," he said, letting his breath out slowly. "I promised Hunter I'd stop back over, but I needed to see you first." He put his hands behind his head and leaned back. "I can't believe this is happening," he whispered. "Who would want to kill my mother, Morgan?"

Morgan stared at him but said nothing.

"None of this makes sense," Carter muttered.

She sat next to him, covering his large hands with her small ones. "How can I help you, honey? Tell me what I can do."

He sniffed. "Help me to make sense out of this," he pleaded.

She softly caressed his hands. "Life doesn't make sense, Carter. It never has and never will. Things like this can never be explained." She drew a deep breath. "I can't stand to see you in such pain," she said as a tear slipped from her eye. "I wish I could take it away."

"There's nothing anyone can do. It won't bring Mom back." He looked into her deep brown eyes. "But at least I have you."

"You'll always have me, Carter," she said quietly.

"And I thank God every day for you."

****

Carter dreamed about being chased through the streets of the city. Every time he ran to a door for help, it slammed shut in his face. Why weren't they afraid of the predator? Or did they believe he was the one they needed to fear? As the enemy grew closer, he ran toward his home. He had to protect Morgan and Becca, they were alone, and he had to reach them before this monster did. His lungs felt like they would burst and he was sweating profusely, but he couldn't stop. He looked over his shoulder just in time to see a large hand reaching for him.

Carter awoke with a jolt and sat up wiping the sweat

from his brow. His heart was thumping erratically and he could barely catch his breath. He drew several long calming breaths before leaning toward Morgan. She was curled up on her side like a baby, fast asleep. He glanced at the clock, it was seven forty-five a.m. He stretched his long frame, dreading what today would bring. He forced himself out of the safety and warmth of his bed and into the shower. He stood under the showerhead letting the water splash down on him.

Forty-five minutes later, Carter arrived at the Craig Funeral Home. He found it hard to concentrate on what Mr. Craig, a small-framed, balding man in his sixties, was saying. He nodded politely as he chose the casket, wondering what difference it would make since there obviously wasn't going to be much if anything to put in it. He made the necessary arrangements, signed the papers, and then assured Mr. Craig that he would call him if he needed any assistance.

Next, he drove to the sheriff's office. He was hopeful that Jake would have some news for him. If he'd had a choice then he wished it had been a gas explosion. At least then his mind could more readily accept an accident over a senseless murder. Maybe Jake would tell him that they caught the bastard who murdered his mother. If he were lucky to have five minutes with the bastard, only one of them would be left when Jake finished with him. He prayed for closure one way or the other and very soon. If not, he didn't know how he or his siblings would ever be able to go on with their lives.

"Morning, Jake," he said, closing the door behind him.

Jake Birch threw down the file he'd been studying. "Good morning, Carter. Would you like some coffee?" he offered.

"No, thanks, Jake. Did you get in touch with everyone? I haven't heard from them." He rested his hands on the sheriff's desk, leaning toward him.

Jake nodded. "Yes, Carter. They're all on their way. I'm surprised they didn't call you." He walked over to the coffeepot, refilled his cup, and carried it back to his desk.

"I'm not. It's no secret that my wife and them are on barely cordial terms."

Jake frowned. "Sometimes it takes a tragedy to bring people together." He sat back down.

"Or to drive them even further apart," Carter said. "Thanks for calling them for me, Jake. You don't know how much I appreciate it." Carter rubbed his chin. "I don't need to ask how they took the news."

"As expected, they were shocked, but mostly because of the circumstances surrounding her death."

"Did they ask why Hunter or I didn't call them?"

"They were concerned that you two were all right, but I think they understood why I called since I've always been close to your family and was calling in that capacity."

Carter exhaled loudly. "Well, thanks again for taking care of it, Jake." He paused. "I don't suppose you have any news?"

"I'm afraid not. It'll take a while to sift through everything."

"You'll let me know the minute anything comes in no matter what?"

"You have my word, Carter."

Carter peered at Jake. "Whoever did this could be long gone from Weldon by now. We might never know who it is."

"Or he may be right here watching us."

"That's hard to believe in Weldon. We're a small tight community. Everybody knows everybody else."

"I've learned in this job that sometimes we don't always know someone as well as we think we do. Sometimes there's a dark side kept hidden from the world."

"That sounds cryptic."

Jake picked up his coffee cup and took a sip. "Take my word for it, Carter, he'll slip up eventually. And when he does, I'll be ready for him. You can count on it."

Carter's eyes narrowed. "What if he doesn't slip up?"

"Someone somewhere knows who did this," Jake stated. "It might take some time but we'll get him."

"You sound confident. Do you have a possible suspect in mind?"

"I wish I did, Carter. I'm just going by what I feel in my gut."

"I hope your gut is right, then," Carter said. He glanced at the clock. "I'd better get home to Morgan. She's going to need to make sleeping arrangements. Hunter doesn't have room for everyone."

Jake patted Carter's back. "Get some rest, Carter. The next few days are going to be rough."

Carter nodded, and then left the office.

Jake watched from his office window as Carter stepped into his car. He felt sorry for him. He wished he could give the man the news he desperately sought, but this was not a case that would be solved quickly. He wished he could alleviate some of the pain Carter was going through, but words would never be enough. It was a senseless crime against a woman who didn't appear to have an enemy in the entire world. Why was Rachel Rogers targeted? There had to be a connection, but what was it? He'd spent most of last night and this morning tracking down leads—all of which lead to dead ends.

He'd known the entire Rogers' clan for over forty years now, but Carter had always been his favorite. His kindhearted nature set him apart from the others. Not that the others weren't decent caring people, but Carter was different. He always looked on the bright side. He never caused any trouble for anyone, not even the boyhood pranks his brothers had been prone to getting into. He'd grown up to be a strong, handsome man, and many young ladies in town had set their sights on him. Jake had thought he'd end up marrying one of them, but he'd met and married a woman who'd probably never even heard of Weldon, Massachusetts until Jake brought her here. His eyebrows knitted together. The residents didn't warm to outsiders right away, but in time they usually did. But not with Morgan. She was different.

She was a looker, though. Jake heard the men around town talking and came to the only conclusion he could—most of them were jealous. Carter Rogers had what they could only dream about. But there was something odd about Carter's bride. She wasn't very sociable and mostly kept to herself. She shunned any attempts at friendship and seemed perfectly content to stay in her own little world with Carter and then their daughter Becca. An odd one there, Jake thought.

****

Carter took his time driving home. He looked at men mowing their lawns while their wives puttered in flower gardens, as children played nearby. This was always his favorite time of the year. The trees were budding, flowers blooming; everything was springing to life — except his mother. She was dead. It was final. He would never hear her voice again. She'd never plant her favorite flowers or vegetable garden. She was gone. It was as though she'd never existed. Everything was gone. All of her treasured family heirlooms and everything else she'd held dear. She was gone, along with the home his father and she had struggled to buy to raise their family. Becca would never know the home he'd grown up in or the grandmother who dearly loved her. She was too young to remember, but he'd make sure she never forgot her grandmother.

A tear fell from his eye and he quickly brushed it away. He couldn't accept her death. He couldn't accept death period. He never wanted to discuss it, but Morgan loved to talk about it. He shuddered every time she brought the subject up. It was morbid. He knew everyone had to face his own demise someday, but that didn't mean he wanted to talk about it when there was so much living to do. He didn't remember ever talking about death to anyone in his family. He'd made the necessary arrangements in the case of his death, but that was as far as he went. He didn't know what provisions, if any, his mother had made in the event of her own. Whatever may have been locked in her safety deposit box inside the house was destroyed. It didn't matter. He and his siblings would take care of any outstanding debts.

He turned the radio on and caught the end of a news story about his mother. "No suspects or leads," the announcer finished, then went on to list his mother's many achievements in the community, and gave the names of him and his siblings.

Carter's thoughts turned to his family.

Paul was the oldest. He and his wife Sarah had two children, Lisa and Terrence. They recently opened a restaurant in Vermont. They both gave up corporate jobs to realize their dream. He hoped they succeeded. They poured all of their assets into their endeavor and knew they were taking a risk, but Paul was certain they could make a go of it.

Collin, the next oldest, his wife Jude, and their three children Sandra, Kurt, and Susie lived in Bangor, Maine. Collin had been station manager at the local TV station until he was offered a position in Bangor. He hadn't wanted to leave Weldon, but the opportunity was too enticing to turn down.

Hunter was next in line, followed by Carter. Six years after Carter's birth, Rachel Rogers gave birth to Raine, then two years later Payton was born. Both of his sisters lived in Portland, Maine. Neither had married.

Carter rounded the corner to his street and pulled into his driveway. Morgan was working in her flower garden. He got out of the car and walked over to her. Just seeing her made him feel better. He was glad she was trying to maintain some semblance of normalcy instead of sitting in the house doing nothing. Doing nothing was, he supposed, the proper way to behave when one was in mourning. But what did it accomplish? Keeping busy helped more than sitting idly dwelling on the loss, which you could do nothing about. How did being quiet help the deceased? They were departed from this earth and he never understood how sitting around for hours crying made anyone feel better.

"Hi, honey." She smiled up at him. "I was worried

about you."

He squatted down to her level. "I made the funeral arrangements, then went to see Jake."

"Any news?" Her eyes searched his face.

"No," he answered quietly.

She picked up a small spade and dug into the moist soil. "I'm sure he'll have something soon."

"I hope so. Where's Becca?"

"I put her down for her nap."

"Okay." He stood and shoved his hands into his pockets. "I hope you don't mind if some of my family stay with us when they arrive."

"Of course not. I expected they would." She stood up and removed her gardening gloves. "We'd better get into the house and make some sleeping arrangements."

****

Carter observed his wife throughout the evening as his family began arriving. She greeted each one sincerely, offering her condolences. She was the perfect hostess, but something was wrong. He could sense it, even though he couldn't put his finger on it. There was a tension in the air. He didn't know the cause of it, but it was definitely there. Suddenly it occurred to him that his family wasn't comfortable around Morgan. They were polite to her, but that was as far as it went. He loved Morgan with all of his heart and soul and wished they would realize once and for all how happy she made him. Couldn't they see that? Shouldn't that be what mattered?

He grabbed a beer from the refrigerator. He popped the tab, and then brought the can to his lips. After taking a large gulp, he set the can on the counter. He was so tired his whole body ached. He stretched, and then yawned.

Collin walked over to him. "Everything arranged, Carter?" he asked in a hushed voice.

"Yeah," Carter answered. He picked up his beer, taking another large swallow. "Did you see Hunter?"

"I just got back from his house. He's in bad shape. Emily called the doctor and he prescribed something for him. He said he'd be over later."

Carter nodded. "Good. I think he needs to be here with his family."

"I agree."

"Want a beer?"

"Yes, thanks."

Carter grabbed another beer from the refrigerator and handed it to him.

"It's hard to stay in control, seeing Hunter like this. It's even worse with the girls." He ran his hand through his hair. "I don't know, Carter," he said in a quivering voice.

Carter put an arm across his brother's shoulders. "We'll get through it. We have to for Mom's sake."

"I know," Collin said, wiping the splatter of tears from his cheek. "It's just the way she died I can't wrap my mind around."

Morgan walked into the room before Carter could respond. "Carter, dinner will be ready shortly. I've got to get everything out of the oven. Why don't you seat everyone, honey? I've set up a card table for the little ones." She squeezed Collin's arm. "It's so good to see you again, Collin, only I wish it were under different circumstances."

Collin nodded and then kissed her cheek. "Thank you

for letting us stay here."

"I wouldn't have it any other way," she replied.

"I'll get everyone to the table, honey," Carter said.

Morgan carried the various dishes to the dining room. When everything was placed on the table, she seated herself. She passed the dishes around while Carter carved the roast.

"You've prepared a feast," Carter said proudly.

"What are we celebrating?" Payton asked sternly. "Mom's dead. Remember?"

Carter noticed Morgan's bewildered expression. "We need to eat," she answered her sister-in-law. "Don't we?"

Payton eyed her coldly. "Cut the act!"

"I don't know what you mean." Morgan frowned as she looked helplessly at her husband.

"Come off it! You never liked Mom! So what the hell are you celebrating—her death?" She slammed her fork down on the table and stood up. "I'm not hungry."

Morgan glanced around at Carter's family. No one said a word and the silence unnerved her. Even the children appeared to be frozen in their seats. Her face grew warm as she choked back tears. She was hurt. No one spoke up in her defense, not even her husband. She looked at Carter again, but his eyes were lowered staring at the roast. Her lips trembled and she immediately left the table and rushed upstairs.

She lay sprawled across her bed sobbing. Why hadn't Carter come to her defense? How could he let his sister talk to her that way? She knew he'd make excuses for Payton's rude behavior. The family always did. Payton was the baby of the family and could do no wrong in any of their eyes. Well, they'd be sorry, she vowed. Every last one of them. Carter would come around. Now that his mother was gone, it was only a matter of time before the rest of the family would unravel. The thick glue that had bonded them was now losing its hold. She turned her head when she heard the bedroom door open. She kept quiet as Carter looking helpless and made his way over to the bed.

"Don't cry, baby," he whispered as he gathered her into his strong arms.

"Why didn't you defend me?" she asked between sobs.

"I'm sorry…I should have, but I didn't want to make a scene. I don't care what any of them say or think. You did nothing wrong."

She looked up at him through tear-swollen eyes. "But I care, Carter. It hurts me. Your family will never accept me no matter what I do. I'm tired of being treated like crap. And I'm tired of you being punished just because you didn't marry someone you grew up with. This town is like a cult. If you're not from here then you'll never fit in."

"That's not true. They just need time to get to know you. My brothers' wives were born and raised here along with us so we already knew them." He paused. "Just give them a chance for my sake."

"How long, Carter? If they don't know me by now, they never will." She reached over to the nightstand table and grabbed a tissue. After she blew her nose, she continued. "Why are you putting it all on me? It sounds to me that you've already taken sides and it's not mine."

Carter opened his mouth to speak, but she placed a slender finger to his lips.

"Don't say anything." Her eyes narrowed. "Let's just get through the next few days."

CHAPTER THREE

Morgan woke early the following morning. She rolled to her side where Carter was sleeping next to her. She softly touched his cheek as she watched him. He looked peaceful. She wondered if he was having a pleasant dream. She kissed his cheek and he stirred slightly but still didn't awaken. She got out of bed and tiptoed into Becca's room. Becca was curled up on her side, thumb in mouth. Morgan bent down and planted a tender kiss on her slumbering daughter's forehead.

She quietly left the room and walked downstairs and into her kitchen. She put the coffee on as she pondered what to fix for breakfast with so many mouths to feed. She took a few packages of bacon and two dozen eggs from the refrigerator and began her preparations.

Her mind wandered to thoughts of her mother-in-law. Tomorrow Rachel Rogers would be buried and after a couple of days, everyone would return to their respective homes and she and Carter could get on with their lives. She smiled. Things would be the way they were supposed to be. It would be perfect now that his mother was gone. Carter belonged to her and only her, and she would make sure that he never even toyed with the thought of leaving her. Even if he wanted to, he couldn't. She'd never let him. She'd tested him a few times to see how loyal he was by threatening to leave *him* and he'd pleaded with her to stay. She'd not intended to leave in the first place, but needed to know that she had him where she wanted him. And she did.

"Mmm, something smells good. What's for breakfast?" Paul asked, breaking into her thoughts.

"Scrambled eggs and bacon," Morgan answered with a smile. "Coffee's ready." She studied her brother-in-law's features as she turned the bacon. He was medium height, on the heavy side, and even though she knew it wasn't very nice, she thought he looked quite repulsive. His personality, although he was a compulsive talker, more than compensated for his homeliness. He kept his naturally curly, sandy brown hair plastered down with gel, making it look greasy and highlighting the dandruff, which at times made him look like he'd just come in from a snowstorm.

Paul poured himself a cup of coffee and sat at the kitchen table.

Morgan wrapped her robe tighter about her body. His eyes were watching her…she could feel it…and it made her nervous. "Did you sleep well?"

"Like a log," he answered as he stretched leisurely. "I still feel like I'm dreaming, though. It's hard to believe Mom's really gone." He sighed dismally.

"I know," Morgan replied quietly. She continued turning the bacon and heard someone else enter the kitchen. She glanced over her shoulder.

"Good morning, everybody," Sarah said with an

obvious forced cheerfulness as she padded into the room. Her furry bedroom slippers made soft swishing sounds on the tiled floor.

"Good morning, Sarah," Morgan answered.

Paul smiled at his wife. "I was letting you sleep in a little, honey. You know you haven't been well lately. Now with all that's happened, I don't want you to become sick again."

Sarah padded over to him, then kissed him lightly on his lips. "Don't worry about me. You have enough on your mind."

What a crock, Morgan thought. Sarah was nothing but a hypochondriac and the way Paul babied her and gave in to her every whim made Morgan want to puke. But of course the family accepted Sarah with no question since she was a local girl. She was brought into their little circle, loved, and treated with nothing but respect. Sarah was the same age as Paul and they had so many similar features one would think they were brother and sister instead of husband and wife. The only difference between them that Morgan could see was that Sarah towered above Paul by a good five inches. She thought it ironic that Sarah and Paul's children turned out to be quite good-looking. Morgan wondered how Sarah had acted during her pregnancies. She imagined Paul must have run himself ragged waiting on her.

"Morgan?"

"Yes?" She turned to Sarah. "I'm sorry. I didn't hear what you said."

"I said is that bacon frying?" Sarah asked.

Morgan wanted to retort, *"What do you think it is, you*

stupid bitch?" but instead said, "Yes, it is, Sarah."

Sarah crinkled up her nose. "Oh. My stomach's a bit queasy this morning. I'll just have some milk toast. I hope it's no bother."

"Of course not," Morgan replied gritting her teeth.

Paul grabbed Sarah's hand. "I'm taking you back upstairs to bed, darling. I'll bring your breakfast up when it's ready."

Morgan continued fixing breakfast as they left the room. Tension crept up the back of her neck and she took several deep breaths to calm herself. She heard footsteps behind her, but didn't bother to see who it was this time.

"Breakfast will be ready in ten minutes," she called.

"Mama, Mama."

Morgan turned around quickly. "Good morning, my precious girl," she cooed as she scooped her daughter into her arms. She planted wet, noisy kisses on her cheek, causing Becca to squeal with delight.

****

Carter laughed as he took Becca from Morgan. He held her in one arm and hugged his wife with the other. "How's it going?" he asked softly.

"Breakfast is just about ready. If I didn't have to make special dishes, it would be a lot easier." She put the bacon on a platter. "Sarah isn't feeling well and wants milk toast," she said rolling her eyes.

He squeezed her shoulder. "Morgan, thank you for doing this for me. I know it isn't easy." He looked into her eyes. The love he felt for her overwhelmed him. He knew how hard she was trying to please his family. He only hoped they appreciated the effort she was making. He placed Becca on the floor, where she quickly waddled over to the cabinet and pulled out pots and pans.

"I'd better get the baby her breakfast," she said. "Can you let everyone know if they want to eat to come and get it?"

He touched her arm. "Wait a minute, honey. I want to talk to you first."

"Is something wrong?" she asked. "Did I do something?"

He put his arms around her, drawing her close, so close he could feel her warm, sweet breath on his neck. "Nothing's wrong," he whispered. "Can't a guy tell his wife how much he loves her?" He bent, and then gently kissed her full lips. "The family wants to go over to Mom's to look around. Maybe we can sneak off by ourselves for a while when I get back."

Becca tugged at Morgan's leg. "Mama, Mama."

"I've got to feed the baby. Would you take the food into the dining room and call everyone to the table before it gets cold?"

"Sure, honey." He picked up the platters.

****

Carter hopped into Collin's station wagon along with the rest of his brothers and sisters. Emily had volunteered to take care of the children while Hunter went with his family to view the remains of the Rogers' homestead. They waited while Collin explained to his children why they couldn't go with them.

"Who killed Gram?" Kurt asked.

"We don't know, son," Collin answered.

"Will he hurt you, too, Daddy?"

34

"No, I'll be fine," Collin assured him as he tousled his hair. "You be good for Aunt Emily."

None of the children had ever been exposed to death before, and Carter wondered how much they actually comprehended. Especially since this wasn't just an ordinary death, but a murder. A part of him was grateful his own child didn't have to be exposed to what his nieces and nephews now endured. When Becca was old enough, he would explain to her what had happened. But that would be a long time off, and hopefully then he'd have the answers he didn't have now.

"Can we go to see Gram with you, Daddy?" Susie asked excitedly.

Carter realized Susie was remembering the stories his mother would tell her grandchildren while munching on freshly baked cookies that she always managed to have waiting whenever they came to visit. He recalled how excited his mother would become every time Collin and Paul announced a weekend visit. How would the children react when they realized that the large house they loved to explore no longer existed? He didn't envy his brothers having to explain that to them, too.

"Gram's gone to heaven, Susie," Collin said softly. "I explained that to you."

Carter turned his attention to his siblings. Hunter sat stiffly like a statue, Payton cried softly, Paul cleared his throat repeatedly, and Raine stared straight ahead with a blank look in her eyes. Carter was concerned about her. She was too quiet and hadn't shown any emotion one way or the other. He decided to keep a close watch on her.

****

Morgan finished loading the dishwasher while Jude wiped down the counter. "It was nice of Emily to watch the kids so they could all play together."

"Yes, it was," Jude replied. "Where's Sarah?" she asked. "I haven't seen her all day."

"Taking a nap. She's not feeling well," Morgan answered, raising her eyebrows.

"I've never met anyone who's had as many sicknesses as Sarah has," Jude said and then laughed. "She really knows how to get out of doing any work."

"That she does," Morgan agreed. "Don't tell anyone, but I heard that the reason Paul decided to go ahead with the restaurant in Vermont was because the company was going to give Sarah the ax," Morgan confided. "She took too many personal days and when she was at work she always complained of not feeling well."

"No!" Her hand flew to her mouth. "Where'd you hear that?"

"I overheard Hunter and Carter talking one night. Paul was put in a bind. I don't believe he intended to open the restaurant for several more years. I hope he can make a go of it financially."

"It's a big risk he's taking."

"He had to save face...well, Sarah's." She frowned. "Just don't breathe a word of it, not even to Collin," she warned.

"I won't," Jude promised.

"Are you taking the kids to the funeral tomorrow?" Morgan asked.

"I'm not sure. We're thinking about taking Kurt. He's old enough to understand, but we're going to find someone to look after Sandy and Susie."

"I'll watch them for you," Morgan offered.

"You're not going?" Jude asked, surprised.

"No, Carter thought it would be best for me to stay here to look after the kids. Besides, I'll have to get everything ready for after the service. We'll have a houseful. All her coworkers from the hospital will most likely stop over along with her church and club friends." She glanced at the clock. "I'd better get Becca up. I want to take her outside for some fresh air." She patted Jude's arm. "You should take advantage of this time away from the kids to take a nap yourself."

"I just might," she replied.

****

Morgan walked slowly through the rooms of her spacious home. Carter had designed this house especially for her. It was like a dream come true. She'd always imagined living in a beautiful house. Marrying an architect didn't hurt either. Carter was one of the best architects in New England, and he'd worked long and hard for that distinction. His company afforded them luxuries they would've only dreamed of just a couple of years ago, but Carter never took his success for granted because a bad year or two could cost him plenty, which was the reason he never struck out on his own. Morgan knew one of Carter's greatest pleasures was fulfilling her heart's every desire. And she was more than pleased to accept.

She admired her large airy living room. She had spent a lot of time and a small fortune picking out each piece of furniture. This was her favorite room of all. The house also contained a large kitchen, family room, den, two baths, and four large bedrooms. Swinging doors divided the kitchen, and the dining room lay at the far end of it.

The full basement had been converted into a recreation room complete with a full bathroom. A long, well-stocked bar took up one wall. In the center of the room stood a standard-sized pool table. Two couches and several easy chairs were centered around a large screen television attached to a wall. At the far end of the basement, Carter had constructed a small village complete with roads, people, and buildings. His trains ran through and around the village on their tracks. Trains were Carter's passion.

Morgan smiled as she picked Becca up out of her playpen. Becca smiled. "Bye-bye! Bye-bye!" she exclaimed excitedly.

"Yes, honey. Mommy's taking you bye-bye."

Morgan carried Becca outside, surprised to see Jude relaxing in a lawn chair. "I thought you were upstairs napping."

"I thought I'd take advantage of this gorgeous weather."

Morgan set Becca on the lawn and surrounded her with toys. Becca stood up. She'd been trying to walk and wasn't very steady on her feet. She took a couple of tentative steps, tottered, and then fell landing on her bottom. She laughed and kicked her feet as she pulled at the cool grass. Morgan smiled at her daughter. She knew that Becca would grow into a beautiful woman. Long beautiful lashes accented her pale gray eyes, and her brown hair was naturally curly.

Morgan took the chair next to Jude's. "It is a beautiful day," she agreed.

"I've been admiring your flower garden. You have a lovely combination!"

"Thank you. Carter and I have been spending a lot of time on the grounds. There's so much we want to do. With two acres, it gives us the privacy we want and space for the baby to play. Next summer he's building a large playhouse for her and putting up her first swing set."

"Knowing Carter, it'll be an entire playground."

Morgan grinned. "He does dote on her."

"Who can blame him? He loves being a father. All the boys in the family are good fathers. Rachel raised them well."

Morgan didn't respond. She was tired of Rachel Rogers being put on a pedestal like she was a saint or something.

Jude's eyes drifted to the new barbeque. "You've certainly done a lot since the last time I was here. Did Carter build the barbecue?"

"Yes. I forgot you haven't seen all of this. We finished it a couple of weeks ago. Now Carter has his own little kitchen outside. He loves grilling." She smiled. "And I certainly don't mind having a night off from cooking. We thought we'd throw some steaks on tonight. Hunter, Emily, and the kids are coming over for dinner and will be spending the night. Carter doesn't want to leave Hunter alone." She frowned. "I was surprised that no one stayed with him and Emily. I thought for sure Raine and Payton would."

Jude was thoughtful for a minute. "Collin told me that Emily was in the middle of a remodeling project. I guess the bedrooms are all torn up."

"That's funny…Carter never said anything to me about it. And they do have rooms in the basement." She looked at Jude. "Well, I'm just happy that we have the room for everyone."

"Me, too. And I thank you for inviting us to stay."

"I wouldn't have it any other way." She leaned back in her chair. "Have you talked to Emily recently?"

Jude sniffed indignantly. "Are you kidding? Have you forgotten that Miss Snob is too good to associate with me? She hasn't changed from our school days and I doubt she ever will. I wonder how's she's taking the death. She was Rachel's favorite."

"I don't know. I haven't seen her or Hunter for weeks. When I do I just ignore her, which isn't hard to do since she only acknowledges me if she has to. She's no better than anyone else, even if she thinks she is. Besides, I have enough problems of my own. I have to contend with Payton. I don't know what I ever did to her, but she treats me even worse than Emily does."

"I never thought I'd want to get away from my hometown, but leaving Weldon was one of the best things that ever happened to us. I don't have to deal with the daily drama of the family."

"Lucky you," Morgan said with a faint smile.

A light breeze rustled the leaves of the large oak tree, and the wind carried the aroma of lilacs in its path. Jude breathed deeply, filling her lungs with the fragrance. "Mmm. I love the smell of lilacs."

Morgan enjoyed the peacefulness of the afternoon, and especially Jude's company. She actually liked Jude and Collin.

Besides Raine, they were the only two people she could truly tolerate in the Rogers family. They didn't ignore her and tried to be friendly. Before they moved, Jude and she had formed a bond. In fact, Jude was the first person Morgan ever considered a friend, and she'd need an ally if she would ever be able to survive in Weldon. Like her, Jude was a loner. But unlike her, Jude was totally introverted and never thought she measured up to anyone. Jude hadn't come from much so that had automatically put her at the bottom in Rachel Rogers' eyes, even though she was a local girl. Still, she was treated better by Rachel Rogers than Morgan, the outsider, was.

Morgan observed Jude as she leaned back in her chair and closed her eyes. She wondered why Jude couldn't see herself in a more positive light. She wasn't a beautiful woman, but she was attractive in her own right. Her eyes were bright blue and she wore her dark blond hair short, but in a style which highlighted her high cheekbones. She was short and slender and was blessed with a complexion that didn't require makeup. There was no reason for Jude to be so self-conscious. And Collin loved her. That was obvious to anyone who saw them together. He looked at Jude the way Carter looked at her.

Of all the brothers, Collin and Carter looked more alike with the same sandy brown hair. They were solidly built and stood six feet two inches tall. The only difference between them was that Carter, in Morgan's opinion, had a much more handsome face.

A bird flew overhead, chirping merrily. Becca clapped her hands together as she squealed, "Mama, bur-die!" Morgan got out of her chair and scooped Becca into her arms for a minute, then set her back down on the lawn where she playfully rolled her in the grass as they laughed together.

CHAPTER FOUR

Carter, along with Paul and Hunter, rushed over to Payton who had fainted. They helped her to her feet. The sight of what had once been their home was too much for her to bear, he thought. She clung to Raine's arm. After he made sure she'd be all right, he moved away from them. He needed his own space right now. Memories came flooding back as he recalled the laughter and joy they had shared as a family. He looked around the debris-filled yard and saw the exact spot he and his brothers had pitched their tents on hot summer nights. He gazed skyward where the upstairs window to his parents' room had once been, remembering fondly his mother yelling down to them to stop their racket or they'd have to come inside. In the side yard had been Raine and Payton's clubhouse, or "girl house," as the boys used to call it.

Payton was closest to their mother. Maybe it was because she was the youngest. He wasn't sure, but she had faithfully called her mother every week and visited twice a month. Being the baby of the family, she was also the last one to leave the family nest. He was surprised she'd even left in the first place.

"Oh God!" Payton mumbled, leaning against Hunter's shoulder. "Why would someone do this?" she cried.

Carter turned and watched Hunter put a protective arm around his sister. He looked in Raine's direction. She poked through the rubble with a stick. Raine always kept her emotions intact. No one could ever be certain what she was thinking or feeling. When their father died she never openly shed a tear. She kept her pain bottled up inside, but this was different. It would have been heartbreaking if their mother had died of cancer, heart disease, or natural causes, but to be murdered was unfathomable. Carter looked closer, squinting. Raine's face was red and he could see tears falling from her eyes, splashing on her flushed cheeks. He started toward her, and then abruptly changed his mind. It was best to leave her alone for now. She needed to work through her grief, but he would be nearby if it proved too much for her to bear.

Carter leaned against a tree, watching his family. They were all so different, yet came from the same womb. He shook his head. He'd never feel the same about anything anymore. He would take nothing for granted, enjoy each day to the fullest, and find peace within himself with no regrets. He needed to seek out that peace. That was the one thing that had eluded him since he took Morgan for his bride. He wished his family would celebrate his happiness. He desperately craved it, but they refused to accept her and that tortured him because family meant everything to him. He knew that Collin's wife hadn't been readily accepted into the family, but since she was a local girl, that was definitely in her favor. That put her way ahead of Morgan. Morgan had been patient believing that someday they would welcome her. To anyone on the outside looking in, it would appear that they had. They were polite, but that's as far as it went. Except for Jude. He was happy when they became close. At least it was a start. At first, Morgan had masked the pain she was feeling from being slighted by the family, but lately she was verbalizing her feelings in ways that made Carter uncomfortable. He knew they were wrong, but he didn't want to lose the closeness he shared with them and he was terrified that eventually Morgan would give him an ultimatum. He sighed wearily. His mind felt like it would explode with the weight on it.

He looked at his brothers again. Hunter was in control of his emotions for the time being. That was a relief to him. It was one thing to see his sisters cry, but he couldn't take it when his brothers did. Tomorrow would be a different story. It would be one of the hardest days he ever had to endure.

Carter waited another ten minutes, and then motioned his family to join him. They stood in front of the car, eyes fixed on the ruins of their former home. The memories would have to suffice now; there was nothing else left. Once again, he felt a tinge of remorse for the part of his life Becca would never experience and for the grandmother she'd never get to know. His stories and photographs would have to be sufficient. All of the family heirlooms and photos of his siblings and him when they were children were gone, too. He was glad that he'd taken pictures of his mother over the years.

After they were settled back in the car, he sat for a long minute and stared at the rubble. "Good-bye," he whispered as he drove away from the house.

The trip back to his house was quiet with everyone wrapped up in their own thoughts. Carter pulled up in front of the sheriff's office. "I want to see if Jake has any news," he explained as he got out of the car.

"Do you want me to go with you?" Collin asked.

Carter shrugged. "If you want to." He peered into the car. "Anyone else?"

The others declined.

The brothers walked into the small office occupied by several filing cabinets with a stack of dusty folders piled on top, and two desks — one for the sheriff, and the other shared by the two deputies who worked with him.

"Good morning, Carter, Collin," Jake greeted them. He threw the newspaper he had been reading aside.

"Morning, Jake," Collin replied. "Carter filled the family in about our mother's death and we're hoping you have some news."

Jake leaned back in his chair. "I'm sorry. Right now it's a cold trail." He picked up a file from the stack on his desk. "This is your mother's," he explained. "It's mostly just pictures. We're not trained for this sort of thing here, but Boston's sending a team of investigators down."

"When?" Carter asked.

"Today." Jake shifted his weight. "Would either of you like some coffee?"

"No, we have to get going," Carter answered, disappointed.

"I'm sorry. I wish I had something to tell you."

Carter looked evenly at him. "What exactly is being done, Jake?" He studied Jake's reaction. He never noticed until now how old the sheriff looked. His hair was so thin that in a few years he'd be completely bald. This case must've really put his nerves on edge since, for as long as Carter could remember, Jake spent most of each day sitting in the park gossiping with the locals while his deputies made the rounds. Nothing much ever happened around here and being sheriff never required much effort. But now that had changed, and Carter supposed Jake was at a loss at how to effectively handle this case. It had set his world whirling. Nothing would ever be the same, nowhere would ever be safe again. The community was shattered. The outside had come in invading their serenity. The serenity he realized they'd all taken for granted. The pride Jake took in having one of the top low-crime communities in the country was gone. His town finally joined the rest of the world, and Jake must be crumbling inside, Carter thought.

"I told you this before, Carter, but it bears repeating. I won't rest until the son of a bitch who did this is behind bars." He threw the folder down. "I'll let you know the minute I have something."

Carter nodded. "Thanks, Jake. I'll be in touch."

"How are the girls holding up?" Jake asked.

Carter grimaced. "Not good, Jake…not good at all." He cleared his throat. "You'll be at the service tomorrow?"

"Of course I will."

"I'll keep my eyes open in case I see or hear anything suspicious. I've heard that sometimes the murderer shows up at the funeral," Carter said.

Collin frowned. "You watch too much TV, Carter."

Jake scratched his jaw. "I don't know. You might just have something there, Carter."

Carter's jaw was clenched as they made their way back

to the car. He knew Jake was out of his league on this one. He doubted much was being done. Jake was right about one thing. He didn't have the resources to handle something like this, but Carter was pissed that the investigators from Boston hadn't been called immediately.

****

Morgan greeted Carter at the door. He looked deeply depressed. Paul and Collin immediately went in search of their wives, and Raine and Payton decided to go for a walk. She led Carter into the kitchen and poured him a cup of coffee.

"Thanks," he mumbled. He stared blankly at the kitchen table.

"What's wrong, honey?" she asked softly.

He pounded his fist on the table. "I'm just discouraged with the investigation."

She rubbed his back. "They're doing the best they can. Jake had no new information?"

"Some investigators from Boston are coming. Hopefully they'll come up with something. I'd just like to know what the motive was," he said bitterly.

"What makes you think your mother was targeted?"

"What makes you think she wasn't?"

She drew a deep breath. "I don't know anything."

He grabbed her hand. "I'm sorry. I didn't mean to snap at you." He looked around the kitchen. "Where's the baby?"

"Napping."

His eyes lit up mischievously. "Would my beautiful wife like to go for a walk with me?"

"And what do you have in mind?" she teased.

"That's for me to know and you to find out."

48

She grinned. "Would you like to see what I'm wearing under my clothes?" she whispered seductively in his ear.

"I can hardly wait," he said pulling her down onto his lap.

Voices outside of the room startled them. Morgan got off his lap and quickly took a chair across from him.

"Hi, girls, did you have a nice walk even though it must have been a very short one?" Carter asked.

Payton shrugged. "We changed our minds."

Raine sat next to Carter, but didn't respond.

Carter looked at Morgan with a questioning look in his eyes.

"I'd better get the baby up or she'll never go to bed tonight," she said, nodding to him. "There's a fresh pot of coffee if you girls want some."

"No thanks," Raine said while Payton shook her head.

Carter frowned. The tension was thick and he wondered what his sisters weren't telling him.

****

Carter woke after a restless night with little sleep. The morning had dawned gray and cold. Rain tapped against the windowpane. He snuggled deeper under the covers, knowing he had to get up but not wanting to. Morgan's even, rhythmic breathing told him she was in a sound sleep. He turned toward her. Her hair hung loosely around her face. She laid on her side, facing him, legs tucked under her like a child. He looked closely at her. Her brow furrowed for a moment but left as quickly as it had come. His lips grazed her cheek. He loved her like he had never loved a woman before and never would again. Becca hadn't altered Morgan's figure or looks, only made her beauty more apparent. She *was* beautiful and she belonged to him. The fact that he was ten years older than her never made a difference to her. She could've had her choice of men, but she chose him. Yes, he was a lucky man. After a proper length of time had passed, he intended to get his entire family together and once and for all clear the air. Morgan wasn't going anywhere and if they refused to accept her, then they refused to accept him. He'd put the pressure on them. They would make the choice. Now that he had that settled, he felt better. Or as good as he could. He still had to get through today. His mouth traveled to Morgan's full lips and he woke her with a deep lingering kiss, which she immediately responded to.

****

Payton looked out of the basement window at the dreary day. Carter had blown up air mattresses for the children to sleep on in one part of the basement and had placed two double cots in another area for his sisters to sleep on. Her brothers and their wives had taken the bedrooms upstairs. She hadn't wanted to stay here, but Emily had no room and Raine had told her it would be rude to get a motel room. She'd reluctantly agreed to stay.

She bit her trembling lip. Today her mother would be buried. She would enter that cold, wet earth. Her mother had enjoyed digging in the earth and planting her many flowers and vegetables. She loved watching the fruits of her labor come to life. How Payton wished her mother could have the same fate after her burial...spring back to life. But she wouldn't be coming back. She was gone for good. There would no longer be leisurely chats on the phone or her mother pampering her when she'd come home for a visit. It was all just part of her memories now. She had no home to come back to.

Payton glanced at her sister's bed. Raine slept deeply and would certainly stay that way for several more hours if no one woke her. She'd never been one to willingly rise in the morning, but would plead for just a few more minutes of sleep. Payton was different. She relished the dawn, opening her arms like a child embracing each new day with the excitement of what it may have in store for her.

Her thoughts turned to Morgan. Even thinking about that woman filled her with an unexplainable rage that at times was almost all consuming. She couldn't remember ever hating anyone like she did her. What had possessed her brother to become involved with Morgan? She believed it to be purely a matter of lust and hoped that when the novelty rubbed off, Carter would realize the error of his ways and relegate Morgan back to where he had found her. It was funny, she thought, no one had ever met a relative or friend of Morgan's. Carter skirted around the issue whenever it was brought to his attention, just as he did whenever the subject of Morgan was brought up, period. In his eyes she could do no wrong. But of course, around him she was the perfect doting wife. She hoped someday he'd open his eyes wide and see Morgan for what she was. She was a lying manipulative bitch. To those she liked, her compliments dripped like honey. But if she didn't like someone, watch out. Her claws would come out, but never where there could be a witness. Payton was heartbroken that Morgan had put a wedge between Carter and his mother and then his youngest sister. And there was nothing she could do about it.

51

Carter had become involved with Morgan when he took a business trip to Pennsylvania to look at some potential development sites for his company. He was gone for several months scouting properties. He wrote frequent letters home about this wonderful woman he'd met. Morgan was a typist for a land development office, and since Carter spent so much time there, it was understandable that they would become acquainted. But Carter's letters said much more than he wrote. He was obsessed with this stranger and emphasized to his family that she was the most compassionate woman he'd ever met. He couldn't wait for his family to meet the woman of his dreams. Payton scrunched up her face, remembering that fateful day he'd brought her home for a visit.

Payton and her mother saw right through Morgan's act by the things she'd say and the look in her eye when Carter left them alone with her. Morgan warned them privately that Carter would never believe anything negative they said about her. She made sure that she was sweet and overly polite to them in his presence. They tried to tell him, but he turned a deaf ear accusing them of not trying to get to know her. They agreed that Morgan's true nature would someday surface and he'd see it with his own two eyes.

Payton often wondered what went on between Carter and Morgan in the privacy of their home. He must have told Morgan what they'd said about her treatment of them since he'd begun distancing himself from the family. Payton wanted to rip Morgan's head off when she'd begun keeping Becca away from her grandmother. She worried about the child. She mostly worried because there was no way that Payton would ever be convinced that Morgan didn't have some mental health issue. She was jealous of anyone who gave Carter too much attention or if Carter gave them too much. Would Becca be punished because of her father's love? Her mother had the same fears. Carter did bring Becca around, though, which at least gave Rachel Rogers some comfort.

Payton found it odd that Morgan never spoke of family or friends and quickly changed the subject when asked by turning the conversation to what was going on in Carter's life. Carter brushed her off whenever she questioned him about Morgan's past or if he'd met any of her family. That didn't matter to him and he'd let her know in no uncertain terms. Morgan had him under her spell and he was mesmerized. Now that her mother was gone, Payton refused to walk on eggshells around Morgan. She would keep silent no longer and she didn't care if Carter liked it or not. Someday he would see that she was only doing it to get him to open his eyes.

She pulled some clothes out of her suitcase and laid them on the cot. She longed for Johnny to be here comforting her right now. She missed him terribly and wished he'd have chosen a different profession, but the Merchant Marines was what Johnny Todd loved and she knew he would never be happy doing anything else. Still, she ached for his strong arms to be holding her right now helping her to get through this intense pain, but she wouldn't see him until fall. That seemed like a lifetime away now.

****

Carter was fixing coffee when Payton walked into the kitchen. "Good morning, honey," he said, turning. Instantly he realized his mistake. "I'm sorry, Payton. I thought you were Morgan," he said.

53

Payton forced a weak smile. "Good morning anyway." She rested her elbows on the counter, watching her brother. "Need any help?"

He shook his head. "I've got it under control, though I doubt it'll taste as good as Morgan's does."

When she offered no comment, he turned toward her. "Are you feeling all right, Payton?" he asked compassionately. "You look pale."

She shook her head. "I'm physically fine, Carter. Emotionally not doing too well. I wish Johnny was here."

"I'm sure he wishes he could be, too."

She twisted a strand of her hair. She used to twist her hair when she was younger whenever she was upset. "I know."

"Why don't you sit down?" He gestured to the table. "Coffee will be ready in a minute."

"Okay." She slowly seated herself.

He checked the pans on the stove, and then pulled up a chair across from her. He looked intently at her. "I think there's something else going on," he stated. "We need to talk about it. You went off on Morgan for no reason the other night. What's going on?"

She clasped her hands together. She wanted to tell him what she really thought, but now wasn't the time. Her mother's funeral was today and she was already drained. "Just forget it."

"No, Payton, I'm not going to forget it. I want to know what the hell is going on with you. I'm trying to help you, dammit!" he said loudly. "Why are you acting like this?"

She smirked. "Maybe, Carter, because our mother was murdered. What do you expect?"

"That's no reason to take it out on Morgan. She doesn't deserve it. Don't you think it's time to let your anger go? Morgan is my wife and if you haven't accepted that fact by now then you never will."

She looked into his eyes. "I don't want to hurt your feelings, Carter, but have you noticed Morgan's attitude about Mom's death? She's shown no sadness."

Carter leaned toward his sister. "I think you know why she's acting the way she is, Payton. She's hurt by the way the family has treated her. Frankly, I don't understand the mistreatment of her. For a long time she kept her feelings to herself, but she finally confided to me what was going on. I tried to keep the peace between her and Mom, but you have to admit Mom didn't treat her very well. I think these past few years have taken a toll on her and now she's letting those feelings out." He grabbed Payton's hands. "But she has never been unkind to anyone in this family. Admit it, Payton. I don't know why you don't like her, but what has she ever done to you?"

"It's not only what she may have said, Carter." She sighed.

"Then what the hell is it?" he demanded.

She shook her head. "I don't know. There's something strange about her. She's so secretive about her past."

He lifted his eyebrows. "No, she's not."

Payton frowned. He wouldn't listen and she wasn't in the mood to get into a debate. "I think we should end this line of conversation. But just remember, Carter, that I care about you. I always have and always will."

"If you care, then please treat my wife with the respect

she deserves," he replied.

She decided to change the topic. "Who's watching Becca this afternoon?"

"Morgan."

She frowned. "Do you think it's wise to bring the baby to the funeral?"

"Morgan's not going."

"What do you mean she's not going?" Payton exclaimed. "Doesn't that prove my point to you?" she smugly asked.

"And what point is that?" Morgan asked, entering the room with Becca tagging behind her.

"Nothing, honey," Carter, flushed, quickly said.

Morgan looked suspiciously at Payton.

Payton caught her eye, and then quickly looked away from the penetrating stare. She forced herself to keep her mouth closed.

"DaDa! DaDa!" Becca ran to Carter, arms waving wildly. Carter smiled as he scooped his daughter into his lap.

"Is everyone else still sleeping?" Morgan asked.

"Yes," Carter answered. "If they don't get up soon, I'll wake them." He returned to his conversation with his daughter. "I've got breakfast started. The coffee should be ready by now, too."

"Good." Morgan poured herself a cup of coffee and then stood behind Carter's chair glaring at Payton.

Payton was frustrated. Of course Carter couldn't see what was going on right under his nose, or in this case, right behind his back. She couldn't even flash Morgan a dirty look because Carter would see.

****

Carter stared down at the freshly dug grave. The heavier rains of this morning had stopped, but there was still a light drizzle with a chilly nip in the air. He barely heard a word Reverend Trasker spoke. All he could think about was that in a matter of moments his mother would be lowered into that dark hole forever. Her life was over. This was final. He wanted to scream at this injustice placed upon her. He gulped, blinking hard as he fought back the urge to cry out in his anguish and pain.

He looked at Payton. Her face was buried in Hunter's arm, her broad shoulders heaving up and down. Emily, silently weeping, clutched Hunter's other arm. Tears poured from Hunter's eyes as he looked at the casket. The rest of the family huddled together in a small group, except Raine. Like Carter, she stood alone. He noticed the frozen, almost expressionless, look on her face. He needed to comfort her. She looked at him. He walked over to her and put his arm around her just as Reverend Trasker asked everyone to bow for a final prayer. Carter lowered his head. He looked up to see his mother's coffin being lowered into the ground. Heart-wrenching sobs broke out all around him. He closed his eyes tightly. He couldn't watch. He held Raine tighter.

Minutes later, he guided Raine to the rest of their family. As they walked to their cars, Jake walked over to them.

"It was a nice service, Carter," Jake said. He uncomfortably shifted his weight from one foot to the other.

"Have you heard anything from the investigators?" Carter asked.

"The Boston team showed up this morning. I know they'll find something, Carter. I'll stake everything I own on it," Jake stated and then hugged him.

Cars began pulling away from the cemetery. More than half the town had come to bid Rachel Rogers a sad farewell. He had always known how loved and respected she was, and this only proved that fact. He looked toward her grave again. He stood silently for a moment. "Good-bye, Mom," he whispered.

CHAPTER FIVE

Weldon had been a prosperous farming community, but the late forties and early fifties saw a swift decline with the coming of manufacturing plants to the area. Some of the farms were replaced with two large textile mills. The mills offered good money for the land, too good for many of the poorer farmers to pass up. Many of them barely made enough to make ends meet and risked losing their farms so the offer for their land gave them a new start. Being conveniently located just twenty miles southwest of Boston gave Weldon the luxury of remaining a quiet rural community as well as the advantage of Boston's culture. Living in Weldon offered the best of both worlds. That's why families rarely moved away.

Aaron Rogers was born and raised in Weldon. After his parents' tragic deaths, when he was an infant, his paternal grandmother Nellie brought him to her farm and raised him as her own. He knew that she was his grandmother, but he still called her Mama. She was the only mother he'd ever known. He'd been a lonely boy with few friends. Most of his time was spent running the farm. He wanted to quit school, but Mama wouldn't hear of it. She insisted someday his education would pay off.

He grew into a strong, handsome man, but loneliness plagued him. He never had time to socialize and lived practically in isolation from the rest of the world. Shortly after Mama's death, he had enlisted in the army. He didn't find the military much to his liking and was relieved when his stint was up. Because he sold the farm before joining the army, he had nowhere to go. He hadn't regretted selling Mama's farm. It had never been much and it would've cost more than it was worth to replace the shack he'd known as home. The soil wasn't good for growing much anymore, and if he'd kept it, he wouldn't have fared any better than Mama. But his dream was to buy a farm of his own and start from scratch. He wanted a farm, which would be prosperous and afford him some luxury instead of just breaking even after breaking his back. He was lonely and desperately wanted a wife and children. Those were the things that would make him complete. That was all he thought about for the four years the army owned him.

He returned to Weldon and purchased a rundown farm at only a fraction of its true worth, but the soil was rich and fertile. That's what mattered. With a little hard work, this farm could be his dream. He would make it his dream. The soil was perfect for growing a large assortment of crops. The buildings, though in bad shape, weren't as bad as Mama's had been. He would make this farm into one of the best in the county. He had the determination and drive.

Five years later his farm was indeed one of the finest in the county. His dreams were materializing. But he still ached with loneliness, and night after night as he gazed at the stars, he prayed to meet someone to share his life with. He knew he wouldn't meet anyone unless he ventured out into the world. He decided one night to get dressed in his best suit and attend the monthly square dance. He continued to attend the dances every month for almost a year and was becoming disenchanted. He'd met many fine women, any of whom would have made him a perfect wife, but something was missing. He felt nothing for them beyond a pleasant chat and a few dances. There was no spark that made him want something more. Maybe he was too picky and should settle for a woman who would bear him children and help him work the farm. As long as they were compatible, they could build a good life together.

One Saturday night as he sat in his usual spot, chatting with a neighboring farmer, his eye caught sight of the most beautiful woman he'd ever seen. "Who's that, Charlie?"

Charlie pulled at his chin. "Damned if I know. Never seen her before, and I sure as hell would remember her!"

"I've got to find out who she is," Aaron said as he stood up.

"What're you gonna do? Just walk right on up to her?"

Aaron eyed him closely. "Do you have any other ideas? I want to meet her before someone else grabs her."

Charlie laughed. "Good luck, Aaron. Send me an invite to the wedding."

Aaron nervously made his way to the woman's table. She watched him curiously as he moved closer. She smiled softly. He self-consciously returned her smile. Her glowing red hair, falling loosely about her creamy white shoulders, made his heart pound with anticipation.

He reached her table, and then mustered up the courage to ask her for a dance. The band was playing a slow song. That was in his favor. He smiled broadly gaining some self-confidence when she accepted his invitation. As he led her to the dance floor, he quickly glanced over his shoulder to see if Charlie was watching. He was and winked his approval.

"What's your name?" he whispered into her ear as he held her in his arms and gently swayed to the music.

"Rachel Wilson," she whispered back. "What's yours?"

"Aaron Rogers." He held her closer, enraptured with the light perfume that had a dizzying effect on him.

He spent the rest of the night dancing and laughing with this beautiful woman. Finally, when the last dance ended, he asked permission to escort her home. She readily accepted. Since that day, they became almost inseparable, and it came as no surprise to anyone when she became his bride six months later.

Rachel fell in love with the farm and soon added her feminine touches to the farmhouse. She possessed a maturity that went beyond her twenty-one years. Aaron supposed that, like him, she had had to deal with loneliness and learn to forage through life on her own. She was an only child and lost her parents in a fire a year before she met Aaron. Her wanderings had brought her to Weldon, the birthplace of her father. Now she knew why her father had reminisced so often about his beloved childhood. But her mother hadn't been content to spend her life on a farm, and persuaded her husband to move to Boston. She was a born and bred city girl and could never be happy living in the country. He gave in to his wife, but Rachel had seen the sadness behind his eyes. She couldn't imagine living anywhere but Weldon.

The years passed quickly, blessing Aaron and Rachel with six healthy children, four sons and two daughters. But after the birth of the first two of their sons, the economy took a downward spiral that hit the farmers the hardest, and Aaron considered selling to one of the mills that were still acquiring land. After many sleepless nights and deliberations, the couple knew they had to do it or risk losing everything they owned. With two children to support, they couldn't take that risk. If it were only Rachel and he, his decision would've been different. Reluctantly, he sold the farm to Bayton Manufacturing Company. He was offered substantially more than he expected for the property and was guaranteed a job as an extra incentive. He bought a large house with a large yard and Rachel and he settled in and added four more children to their family. They were happy and content once again. He worked in the plant until his death. He justified it in his own way; at least every day when he walked into the plant he would still be a part of the land he had so loved.

****

Carter sighed and closed the magazine he had been thumbing through. It was an old copy published years ago by the members of his mother's women's club. His mother wrote the piece on his parents. Every member of the club had their story published. No one outside of their club received or read the magazine, but it was still a testament of their life together. He was glad that he'd taken the magazines home to read some time ago. He'd never gotten around to reading all of the stories, but had promised his mother he'd return them soon. Now he was relieved that he hadn't or they, too, would be gone. He set the magazine aside as he wondered who would've wanted to end his mother's life. Two weeks had passed since the funeral and still not one clue.

He walked over to the window, gently pushing the drapes aside. Morgan pulled weeds in the vegetable garden. Her flowered gardening hat was perched precariously on top of her head. Becca gleefully sat at her side, laughing as she pulled at imaginary weeds. Carter watched his wife and daughter for a long time, feeling a warmth surge through him at his good fortune to have found Morgan. He wondered if it was the same feeling his father had felt when he had found his wife. It must have been. Like his father, it took the right woman to make him come alive.

****

Emily started to toss the salad. Suddenly a large hand clamped itself over her eyes, and she smiled, smelling the faint scent of Hunter's aftershave.

"Guess who?" his deep voice teased.

"Hmm, let me think for a minute," she said. "Oh, I know! It has to be my secret lover!"

"Secret lover, huh!" Hunter feigned shock. He swung her around until she was facing him. "Hi, sweetheart," he whispered. He tenderly kissed her lips.

"Sounds like you had a good day." She caressed his cheek.

"It wasn't bad," he answered as he grabbed a beer from the refrigerator and then seated himself at the counter.

She noticed how haggard he looked. The past two weeks had taken an enormous toll on him. He'd lost weight and his once broad, erect shoulders now had a slight slump to them. The night after his mother's funeral, she had held him throughout the night as he finally cried, releasing some of his pain. Two hours before dawn, finally exhausted, he fell into a fitful sleep. He hadn't slept much in the past two weeks. He pretended to sleep, but several times Emily woke in the night to find the space beside her empty. She'd spot him staring out of the window into the darkness. She allowed him his space. He needed to come to grips with this tragedy in his own way and for however long it took. He knew she'd be there beside him when he needed to lean on her.

She smiled at him. "How are you feeling, Hunter?" she asked softly.

He stretched his long legs. "A little tired." He set his beer on the counter. "I was thinking about going to the lake this weekend if the weather's nice. We could have a cookout." He blew his breath out. "I need to get away even if it's only for a day."

"That sounds like fun. The kids will love it."

His eyebrows knitted together. "We could ask Carter and Morgan to come along." He looked at her. "If you don't mind. Maybe it's time we all buried the hatchet."

"You're right," she agreed. "Maybe I can even get Morgan to give me some swimming lessons."

"She is a good swimmer, you know."

"Yes, I know. I've seen her swim," she replied. "How many times has the family been to the lake? Everyone gathers around to watch her."

He laughed. "Ouch! Are those claws?"

She playfully poked him. "Stop it, Hunter Rogers. If

you're insinuating that I'm jealous of Morgan just because she is such an accomplished swimmer, then…" She leaned closer to him until her face was directly in front of his. "You're right," she finished with a laugh.

"I knew it!"

"Well, I can't help it." She walked back to the stove. "I'll give Morgan a call later to invite them."

"Good. I hope they can make it."

"I do, too."

He got up, and then walked over to the salad bowl, grabbing a piece of carrot.

Emily moved over to him and playfully slapped it from his hand.

"Hey!" he yelped as the carrot fell back into the bowl. "I'm starving." He picked the piece of carrot back up and popped it into his mouth.

She shook her head. "Sometimes I think you're worse than ten kids."

"And you love it," he replied.

"When's dinner, Mom?" Justin asked, bounding into the room. He set the basketball he clutched in his arms on the floor and started bouncing it.

"In fifteen minutes." She turned toward her son. "Justin, how many times have I told you not to bounce that ball in the house?" Her voice was stern.

"It's called dribbling, Mom," he explained.

"Well, I don't care what it's called, please refrain from doing it."

"Okay, sorry." He picked the ball up into his large hands.

Emily smiled at him as she ruffled his fuzzy light brown hair. "It's okay. Just try to remember." He didn't have many friends even though he had an outgoing personality. Kids poked fun at him because of his size since he towered over them. He was overweight, and she knew it bothered him even though he never said anything to her, but his eyes gave away what he felt. Now she looked into those deep-set, beautiful brown eyes and was aware of the loneliness in them. He was only eight years old but looked at least twelve. She knew she was to blame for letting his weight get out of control, but she could do nothing about his height. Someday the other boys would catch up to him. She made a mental note to start paying more attention to his diet. "Why don't you see if your father will shoot some hoops with you after dinner?"

His eyes lit up as he turned to Hunter. "Will you, Dad?"

"Of course I will, sport," Hunter promised.

"Daddy," Beth yelled, racing over to her father.

Hunter scooped her into his arms. "How's my princess?" He balanced her on his shoulders. "Want a piggyback ride?"

She squeaked with delight. "Yes, Daddy!" She giggled as Hunter stomped around the kitchen. She wrapped her pudgy arms tighter around his neck.

Looking at Beth brought to mind a comment Payton told Emily she'd overheard Morgan make the day of the funeral. Payton had been sitting in the kitchen when Morgan remarked to Jude how overweight Beth was. Then Payton listened in shock as Morgan made fun of Beth's long brown hair, calling it mousy. But the ultimate came when Morgan said Beth was the ugliest little girl she'd ever laid eyes on. Emily's facial muscles tightened. How could anyone make such cruel remarks about a child? No normal person would. But in Emily's mind, Morgan was far from normal. Still, she had to put her personal issues with Morgan aside. It was a well-known fact that Payton couldn't stand Morgan and possibly exaggerated what was really said. She'd give Morgan the benefit of the doubt for Hunter's sake. He needed to spend time with his brother, so she'd bite the bullet and try to get along with Morgan. Asking her for swimming lessons was the first step.

CHAPTER SIX

Payton peered into her refrigerator, but not feeling particularly hungry, she pulled out a bottle of diet cola. She grabbed some ice cubes, placed them in a glass, and then poured the cola over them. She picked up her drink and carried it into the living room where she plopped herself down on the sofa. She gazed around the untidy room, debating whether she should clean it up. She decided to let it wait. She was tired. She looked around for the TV remote and finally found it under a stack of week-old newspapers. She flicked on the set and settled for the evening news.

The apartment was unbearably stuffy tonight. She got up and threw open the two windows, then looked at the thermometer outside of the window. Eighty degrees. She pulled her shoes off, and then struggled out of her sticky panty hose. She took another large swallow from her drink. She should really get a window air conditioner, she thought as she flicked on the fan.

Carter and Morgan's impending visit next month bothered her. Carter had called her out of the blue last night asking if she'd mind them coming for a visit. He assured her if it was too much of an imposition then he would book a hotel room. Portland, Maine wasn't that far from Weldon so it had puzzled her that they were intending to spend the night until he explained that there was a two-day art festival Morgan wanted to go to. Payton didn't know if she could stand a whole day and night with Morgan in such close proximity. But she'd do it. She loved spending time with her brother and niece.

Carter had emphasized that it was Morgan's idea to ask to stay with her. He'd hinted that this was Morgan's way of trying to get to know her sister-in-law better and put the past behind them. He hoped that Payton would meet her halfway. As he explained, Morgan and she had never spent much alone time together since they only saw one another at family functions, so this was the perfect opportunity for them to really talk and clear the air.

Payton wasn't aware of Morgan's interest in art and Carter had admitted that he was as surprised as Payton at her sudden interest, but he had promised her that he'd take her to the art show. She assured him that the visit would be fine, but inside she was dreading it. What was Morgan really up to? And why the sudden interest in art? Payton didn't trust her for one minute. Morgan had another agenda. They would have stayed with Raine if she had the room, but she lived in a small studio, the same one she'd rented in her sophomore year of college. She'd fallen in love with Portland and after college decided to stay. She'd worked her way up to manager in an exclusive jewelry store. Two years later Payton had enrolled in the same college. It hadn't taken her long either to fall in love with Portland. The sisters had decided, against their mother's wishes, to live apart since they'd grown up sharing a room. They explained that they both needed to be out on their own, but would remain as close as they always had been. Nothing could ever put a wedge in their sisterly bond. That was until Morgan entered the picture. They'd never argued as much in their entire lives as they had in the past few years.

Her lips puckered. Carter and Morgan had never even visited her apartment. No, there was something very fishy about this. When she'd met Raine for lunch today and told her about Carter's phone call and her suspicions regarding the visit, instead of listening to Payton's concerns, Raine jumped down her throat, calling her a troublemaker and accusing her of wanting to destroy her brother's marriage.

"I don't want to destroy his marriage, but something's not right with her. She treated Mom and me like crap, but of course never when anyone could witness it," Payton retorted.

"For God's sake, Payton, stop finding fault with everything she says and does," Raine said. "They're so happy together. Maybe if you took the time to get to know her you might find out that she really is a sweet person. And she loves Carter with all her heart."

"Sweet?" Payton smirked. "She's so sweet she couldn't even be with her husband at his mother's funeral!" She grimaced.

"I don't blame her! I loved Mom with all my heart, but face the facts, she never gave Morgan a chance. From the day they met, Mom found fault with her. I never knew Mom to dislike anyone before Morgan."

"That's because no one ever gave her cause to."

"I might have been able to justify Mom's dislike of

71

her, if I would have seen or heard Morgan saying some of the things Mom and you accused her of." She eyed her sister coldly. "But I didn't."

Payton pursed her lips. "Mom and I know her true nature!" she insisted. "Maybe someday you will, too, Raine."

They'd finished their lunch and tensely went back to their respective jobs.

Payton stretched out on the sofa. They'd make up just like they always did. They'd always been close. In fact, the whole family was tight-knit. The only time the family began to unravel was when Morgan joined them. Payton had tried to like her, but it was impossible. No one saw the nasty side of Morgan. Well, almost no one. Lately Emily had mentioned to Payton privately that Morgan had made some sarcastic remarks to her. Emily kept quiet, but it was only to keep the peace. No one in the family knew anything about Morgan or where she'd really come from. She kept her past locked up tightly. Payton was saddened that Morgan had come between Carter and their mother. Why couldn't Carter see it? She was tearing their family apart. Her private digs were cruel, but she had Carter wrapped around her little finger.

Jude was the only one who had taken an immediate liking to her upon their first meeting. But then Jude had always had a slight chip on her shoulder, Payton reasoned. She'd felt like the family didn't accept her as willingly as they had Sarah and Emily, which was complete nonsense. Jude was a local girl, but her family was poor so Jude naturally thought Mrs. Rogers held that against her, which she never had. Payton supposed Morgan used that to bring Jude into her web.

Payton knew that in the end, though, all of the siblings would have one another's backs. Their mother had always told them to remember that blood is thicker and to always stay true to your family. She knew she'd have each of their backs if the need ever arose just like they'd have hers. And that's exactly what Raine couldn't seem to understand. Payton had Carter's back while the rest of them were oblivious to what was happening right under their noses. Morgan bore watching.

****

Paul sat at his desk, feverishly totaling the night's receipts. Sarah set a steaming cup of coffee on the desk.

"Thanks, honey." He glanced up, and then quickly went back to his task.

"Paul?"

"Huh?" he answered distractedly as he penciled a figure in the book.

"Why do Carter and Morgan want to come for a visit over Labor Day weekend?" she asked skeptically. "Doesn't it seem odd to you?"

He shrugged and set the pencil down. "Not really. They've been promising to visit for the past two years, but something always seemed to come up. I think Mom's death has made Carter realize how important family is. He hasn't been in contact with the family much since he got married." He picked up the cup of coffee and took a sip. He peered at his wife. "Now don't you get on Payton's bandwagon and blame Morgan."

"There's something about her, Paul. Maybe your mother and Payton know something about her that we don't."

"Come on now." He chuckled. "They refused to accept her for one reason only. She wasn't from Weldon. If she was, then they would know every little detail of her life. It frustrated them that she wouldn't give them any details."

"Don't you find that odd?"

He cocked an eye. "No. It's none of my business. She could have had a painful childhood and doesn't care to rehash the details of her life."

"You could be right." She sighed. "But something doesn't feel right about their visit." She picked up her knitting basket and walked to an easy chair across the room, but didn't sit down.

"I thought you wanted them to come, Sarah."

"I do. It's just this feeling I have, Paul. I can't put my finger on it, but it's nagging at me." She set her knitting basket down.

"Come on, honey. You're just upset over Mom. We all are." He got up from the desk and walked over to her. He put his arms around her. "We'll have a great time. Just wait and see. Besides, it'll give me a chance to show off our restaurant."

"I know I'm being silly, but it seems like their making the rounds visiting the family. They've never done that before."

"Who else are they visiting?"

"Payton called earlier and said they're going to the lake this weekend with Hunter and Emily and then are planning a visit with her and Raine, and now they want to come here."

"It's like I said. I think Carter wants to reconnect with the family and Morgan is making an effort to really get to know everyone. It's too bad that it took Mom's death to bring Carter back to the fold."

"Speaking of your mother, when Carter called, did he have any news about the investigation?"

"No." Paul frowned. "I'm beginning to think we'll never know who killed her or why."

CHAPTER SEVEN

Jake Birch frowned. "I don't follow you." He looked sharply at the man seated across from him. Mark Barlow was one of the investigators Boston had sent to investigate the Rogers case, and that in itself was reason enough for Jake to mistrust him. He'd never confided this to anyone, but he was angry he hadn't been able to solve the case on his own. If he had, he envisioned the public outpouring of accolades at the fine way he took care of his town. But no, he hadn't even been able to come close. Now this outsider, this big shot, was going to tell him how to do his job when after several weeks they hadn't come up with anything either.

"It's very simple, Sheriff. Whoever killed Rachel Rogers probably won't stop with her death."

"It seems like he has. You see how quiet it's been."

"He's waiting to make his next move." Barlow was thoughtful for a minute. "He's sending a message."

Jake almost laughed out loud at the notion, but controlled the urge. "And just what is that message?" he asked with a touch of sarcasm in his tone.

"That this is only the beginning."

"Of what?"

"I think something happened — could be years ago or recent — that involves one of the Rogers'."

"That's ridiculous," Jake said dismissing him. "I've known that family for years. I watched those kids grow up. Not one of them has so much as gotten a speeding ticket."

"Could be an act of revenge," Barlow continued.

"Revenge?" Jake scoffed. "Rachel Rogers didn't have any enemies to speak of."

"Maybe you don't know the family as well as you think you do. All families have secrets."

"Not this family," Jake answered confidently. "You seem to forget Weldon is not Boston."

"I'm well aware of that."

"Any other theories?" the sheriff asked, seemingly amused with the investigator. "You're ruling out a random act of violence?"

"If it was a random act, why would he hit just one house? Why not somewhere he could take out a group of people like a restaurant or the community center? No, I think Rachel Rogers was targeted and it's up to us to find out why."

"If what you say is true, no one around here has noticed any strangers in town. Believe me, around here everybody knows when his neighbor takes a shit."

A smiled tugged at the corner of Barlow's mouth, but he quickly regained his composure. He walked over to the coffeepot and poured himself a fresh cup. "It could be a local…someone familiar enough with Rachel Rogers to know every inch of her home and her comings and goings."

"That would make almost everyone in town suspect."

"Or it could be someone who's moved away and has come back."

"The word would have been out."

"Well, since you stated you know everyone in town, is there anyone who acts abnormally or could be considered mentally unstable, but considered harmless? Possibly someone one of the Rogers may have had an issue with?"

Jake's jaw tightened. "Sounds like you're grasping at straws." He leaned forward staring evenly at Barlow. "There's no one in town who fits that description. And for the record, the only incident of anyone acting odd we have around here is Mrs. Martin, a retired history teacher, but she's harmless. The worse thing she's ever done is run naked through the streets screaming, 'The British are coming.' She's currently in the nursing home unable to get out of bed."

"My instincts tell me it'll be someone you least suspect. Someone right under your nose."

Jake studied the man. He hoped Barlow was wrong. Barlow looked sharp in his expensive-looking tailor-made suit. Jake figured him to be at least fifteen years his junior. He was tall and lean and his twenty years of experience definitely gave him the edge. Boston had sent their best man. Jake rubbed his chin. "I still can't think of anyone in Weldon capable of murdering that woman."

"What about someone in her own family?"

Jake almost choked. "Now that's really grasping at straws."

"It happens more than you know."

"Maybe in Boston, but not here."

"Did she ever have a tiff with any of her daughters-in-law

that you can recall? You stated she has three."

Jake's eyebrows shot up. "You've got to be kidding me if you think one of them would have harmed her."

"Stranger things have happened. They could have hired someone to pull it off."

"No, that's ridiculous. They are local girls and I personally know them and their families." He paused. "Wait a minute. Her youngest son Carter married a girl from Pennsylvania."

"Do you know her well?" Barlow persisted.

"I don't know much about her," he admitted. "Still, what motive would she have? I've seen the entire family together at community functions and there was nothing unusual about her. There's no way I'd ever suspect her of having anything to do with Rachel Rogers' death."

He nodded. "I understand. But it wouldn't hurt to keep an eye on this daughter-in-law. Stranger things have happened."

****

Morgan tucked a blanket around Becca and then walked to the window and looked out at Carter who was watering the large vegetable garden.

A few minutes later she slipped into the den, silently closing the door behind her. She sat in the darkness and gathered her thoughts. Her dreams were finally beginning to come true. A year ago, she painstakingly put her plan into motion. She had been patient, knowing the outcome would be well worth the wait. Now her hard work was finally paying off. No one would ever stand between her and the man she loved. She scowled. No one would ever mistreat or abuse her again. She wouldn't put up with it anymore. She'd taken too much, more than one person deserved, but now the revenge would finally be hers. She had waited a long time for this and now that she was seeing the fruits of her labor, she was giddy with excitement.

She'd been born into a large family, a family she had not asked to be born into and often wondered why she was. Raised in Minnesota on a large farm with her five brothers and four sisters, she'd never felt the sibling bond the rest of them had. In fact, she never even felt a parental bond. She painfully realized at an early age how unfair and unjust the world really was. If you weren't wanted in a circle, then you were kept out. But it hurt worse knowing her family had locked her out of their circle, a circle she should have been welcomed into at birth. She spent her first eighteen years of life locked in her own personal hell of loneliness, wondering if she would ever fit in anywhere. People were hard to get close to. No one seemed to understand what she was about, so most avoided her, thinking her an oddity. She shielded herself from this cold world by voraciously reading everything she could get her hands on. It was her only escape into a world where parents loved all their offspring equally, and even though the siblings would have their occasional squabbles, deep down the love and acceptance was evident. She yearned for their lives, but it was never to be for her.

She existed but didn't live. She saved every dime, squirreling it away in a secret savings account. The day after her high school graduation, she drew her money out of the bank, and then walked to the bus station carrying a tattered suitcase that held her few worldly possessions. She bought a ticket bound for Pittsburgh. If she planned carefully, she'd have enough money for a cheap room and a few meals while she hunted for a job.

On the long bus ride, she looked forlornly out of the window, knowing she would never see her family again and not really wanting to. They hardened her against this world she lived in, but they taught her one valuable lesson—go after everything you want and don't care who you hurt in the process. She was incapable of loving anyone. She wasn't even sure what being in love was all about. She'd never been exposed to the security of a family's warmth and love. She had never known the feeling that came from a tender hug or a kind word. These things didn't exist in her world. Now on the bus, she felt like she had just been let out of prison. And in a strange way she had.

When the bus pulled up to the Pittsburgh terminal she climbed off, not knowing which way she would go, and blindly walked the streets until a kind police officer stopped her and explained the dangers of walking alone at night in a large city. He led her to an inexpensive but safe rooming house, where she wearily laid her tired head on the pillow and slept deeply for the next twelve hours. She woke refreshed and with determination to finally begin her life. The next two days she walked through block after block of businesses, submitting application after application. It didn't look promising. The job market was in a decline with unemployment on the rise. Dejectedly she walked back to her tiny room, wondering what she would do when her money ran out.

Just when it appeared she faced her darkest hour, a phone call came for her. A land development company was willing to hire her on a trial basis. She grinned as she hung up the phone. She'd work hard and prove to them that she was worth hiring permanently. She stayed to herself, not socializing with her coworkers. She didn't trust them. They seemed friendly enough, but it wasn't a chance she wanted to take. She was better off on her own. She worked day after day, week after week, and found peace. She'd distanced herself from the sad, abused little girl she'd been for eighteen years back on the Minnesota farm.

When Carter Rogers came into the office one day everything suddenly changed. She didn't want to become friends with him, but he seemed different from everyone else. Maybe he sensed she was like him. She didn't know. But she surprised herself by looking forward to his visits and friendly chatter. Still, she was scared. He seemed to like her, but could he love her? She wasn't sure anyone could. She'd been told so many times throughout the years that she was unlovable that somewhere in her subconscious mind it became the truth. But now this kind, handsome stranger wanted to spend time with her. She had to hold back because if she didn't, just when she made herself vulnerable, he'd pull the carpet out from under her. As cautious as she was, she couldn't stop the feelings she was developing toward him. For the first time in her life, she felt the real stirrings of love. She'd thought she'd felt those feelings long ago, but then things had abruptly changed and she'd been hurt and then realized it hadn't been love at all. Those people couldn't hurt her again. She'd seen to that. She vowed to never tell Carter about her family. If she did, he might not want to see her again, and that was a pain she just couldn't bear. It was safer to have no past. She would never let her past catch up to her.

But still, there was a major obstacle with their budding relationship. Carter had a family — a family he deeply loved. He couldn't give all of his love to her. She had to share it with them. She wouldn't have minded if his family had given her some of their love, too, but they couldn't. She didn't fit in. They were friendly enough, though they had a circle too, and like her family, wouldn't let her in. She stood on the outside watching as they snatched Carter from her and brought him into the circle, and then quickly joined hands to form a strong chain she couldn't penetrate. Carter seemed happy within the circle and didn't seem to mind that she was excluded. She thought about punishing him, but she loved him too much. Besides that, he was good to her and he was the first person in her life to show her what real love was. No, she needed him. It was better to have one person to love you than go back to the loneliness that had been her life. His family brought out her insecurities and she was terrified that they might someday convince him to leave her. She would never let that happen. She'd never let him go or let anyone get between them. All she had to do was keep a close watch on the family.

She sighed. It took a lot of energy, but it was worth it to keep him close. As for happiness, she knew it would never truly be hers. She'd figured that out a long time ago. Happiness and peace would never be a part of her life, but as long as she had Carter totally on her side, she would survive. Without him, she would succumb. She was terrified that certain members of the family who didn't like her would never give up their quest to convince him to leave her. She had to keep him away from those who said cruel things about her. Lately Carter had been pushing her aside and not seeming to care about her feelings. He'd said nothing to Payton when she attacked her without provocation a few weeks ago. Could he already be listening to them? Maybe she'd been so busy with the baby that she hadn't caught the signals. She had to stay alert and stick to a plan. She couldn't rush it or someone might catch on. Morgan knew what she had to do about Payton, though. She sighed. Everything she did was for Carter and someday he would see that. She loved him that much. When they were finally rid of the encumbrances of his family, she would explain it to him. He would realize that what she'd done was the only thing she could have done, and he would be grateful to her. They could live their lives together in peace without anyone trying to erode their happiness.

She closed her eyes. June was such a lovely month, her favorite. Summer was in the air. The flowers bloomed and her vegetable garden was sprouting. She wondered if it was her favorite month because that was when she had left Minnesota, or had it always been her favorite month. She couldn't remember, but it didn't matter. Her mind drifted to Saturday. Why had Emily called and invited them to the lake for a barbecue? She didn't like Emily and the feeling was mutual, but Carter insisted they go. She would only go because Carter asked her to and she'd do almost anything he asked her because he asked so little. He'd actually done her a favor by accepting the invitation, though, and all she had to do was slightly change her plans around a little. Her adrenalin began pumping with anticipation.

She smiled and rubbed her palms together enjoying how everything seemed to be falling into place for her. Several weeks ago Carter had to go out of town on business. It was the break she needed to set her plan in motion. She drove to a debris-littered street in Dorchester. She couldn't risk purchasing the items too close to home. As she parked the car, she was well aware that she was risking her own life coming into the neighborhood but she had no choice. She sat in the car for a minute gathering her courage as she looked at the graffiti-painted rundown buildings. A group of teens stood on the corner and made obscene gestures at her. She got out of the car, locked it, and then hurried into one of the buildings, grateful that the youths didn't move from their corner. She hoped the car would be intact on her return. Her heart thumped wildly as she explained to the little dog-faced man behind a counter what she sought. He grabbed the items and she paid him in cash and then hurried out of the building and back to her car. The teens were gone and the corner was empty. Still, she didn't feel safe until she was locked inside. She breathed a sigh of relief, started the car, and headed for home.

She called Rachel on the sixth of May, inviting her for a visit with the baby. She knew Rachel would be surprised at her invitation but would also jump at the chance to spend time with Becca. She was crestfallen, though, when her mother-in-law told her she couldn't make it that evening. Luck shined on Morgan, however, when Rachel informed her that the reason was because Hunter and Emily had invited her to dinner that same evening. She'd asked if she could visit with Becca the following day, a day only Morgan knew Rachel Rogers would never see, so Morgan readily agreed. Morgan had already made a copy of her mother-in-law's spare key, which Carter kept in case of an emergency. She'd sneaked it from his key chain one night as he slept and replaced it before he knew it was even gone.

That evening after dinner, Morgan made an excuse to leave the house. She told Carter she needed to run to the store to pick up some diapers for the baby.

"I'll go," he offered.

She wrapped her arms around his neck. "You've been working hard all day, honey. Just relax and keep an eye on the baby. There are a few other things I should pick up. It'll save me a trip to the supermarket tomorrow."

"Okay." He kissed her.

She grabbed her purse.

"Hey, I've got an idea," Carter said suddenly. "Why don't we all go? Becca can get some ice cream."

Her heart thudded. She needed to think of something quick. "No...her stomach's been upset today. I don't think she should go out," she lied.

"You're right. She shouldn't go then." Carter picked Becca up and held her in one arm. "I guess it's just you and Daddy for a little while," he said.

Ten minutes later, she was driving through her mother-in-law's quiet neighborhood. She circled the block twice, making sure no cars were in Rachel's driveway. She carefully observed the neighbors' houses, noting the closed blinds. The street was silent. That's the way it always is around here, she thought. They go to bed with the chickens and get up with the roosters.

She drove two blocks from the house, and then parked her car in front of a housing development. Morgan got out of the car and looked around. No one was in sight. She walked down the block and then turned at the adjoining street, stopping where Rachel's backyard abutted her neighbors. She quickly glanced around, and then stole into the darkened backyard. She panted as she made it to the back door and then quickly let herself inside. Morgan tiptoed to the stairs and slowly climbed them. Exhilaration mounted within her. Her heart pounded with joy as she reached the master bedroom door. Laying her hand on the doorknob, she took a few seconds to gaze at the familiar layout and wondered how many times, as a child, Carter ran to this room for comfort when something had frightened him. She'd been scared many nights as a small child, but she was never consoled and stayed huddled under her blanket, fearing the demons she was sure were out to get her. Morgan threw her head back as if shaking away her unpleasant memories and then opened the door and slipped inside. This had to work. She hadn't considered the possibility that it wouldn't. She'd made several phone calls to various agencies out of state explaining that she was writing a mystery novel and wanted to get the details correct. The specialists were more than happy to help her out and she'd promised to acknowledge them in her book and send a copy along when it was published in exchange for their assistance. She unplugged the bedside lamp and carefully inserted a device, and then connected the wire to the timer switch. She set the timer for nine p.m. Rachel Rogers would be home and preparing for bed. She always prepared for bed at nine p.m. sharp.

Morgan smiled, remembering, and then shook her memories aside. This was the present. She walked out to the backyard. Carter grinned and playfully aimed the hose in her direction.

****

"Hey, get me a beer somebody!" Hunter yelled as he dumped charcoal into the grill. He pulled his shirt off and wiped sweat from his brow.

Emily pulled a can of beer from the cooler. "Justin, take this to your father, please."

Justin obediently ran to his father and handed him the can of beer. "When we gonna eat, Dad? I'm hungry."

"Not for a while, Justin." He tousled the boy's hair. "Go tell your Uncle Carter to get his ass over here."

"Sure, Dad," Justin replied.

Hunter eyed his son. "But leave out the ass part."

The boy laughed. "Okay."

Hunter stretched out on the grass, gazing up at the bright cloudless sky. He drowsily closed his eyes.

"Got the coals started, I see," Carter said as he stood over him and then sat on the grass next to where Hunter lay.

Hunter yawned, then sat up. "Yeah, if you hadn't gotten over here I may have fallen asleep." He took a large gulp of beer. "What are the wives up to?" He hoped they were getting along. After the tragedy, he'd hoped it would bring the family closer.

"Morgan's going to give Emily a swimming lesson shortly. I said we'd look after the kids and take them swimming later on." He sipped at his beer.

Hunter sighed. "We should make the kids stay over here so they don't watch." He looked at Carter. "Emily's embarrassed that she doesn't swim well."

Carter shrugged. "She shouldn't feel that way."

88

"I know. I've told her that a thousand times, but it still bothers her." He pulled at a blade of grass. "She has a fear of the water, but she won't talk about it. In fact, very few people know about it. She'll go in the water with the kids, but it takes every ounce of courage for her to do so."

"I didn't know that." Carter said.

"Don't let anyone know."

"I won't. Hopefully Morgan will turn her into a good swimmer and she'll lose her fear."

"I hope so. It won't be long until Morgan teaches Becca."

"She'll have to start soon," Carter replied. "I can't keep that one out of the water." He smiled. "Her bath time grows longer each night. She refuses to get out of the tub."

"It could be worse," Hunter warned. "Beth used to put up a fight at bath time for the opposite reason."

They drank their beers in silence for a few minutes.

"So, what's the news on the investigation?" Hunter finally asked. "You hear anything? Jake said he's been meeting with the investigator, but he wouldn't tell me anything. Do you think he knows something?"

Carter shook his head. "I don't know. I really think he'd tell us if he did."

"Well, we'll just have to make sure that Mom's case isn't put on the back burner and turned into an unsolved cold case."

"It never will be. I'll see to that," Carter affirmed. "One way or the other I want answers. We deserve that much."

"Mom deserves that much," Hunter stated firmly.

"That she does." Carter finished his beer.

****

"Here come the wives," Hunter said forty-five minutes later. "It sure took them long enough." His eyes stayed focused on Emily's red bikini-clad form moving toward him.

"You know women." Carter chuckled. He looked at his brother who still had his eyes glued on his wife. After all these years, the love they shared was still evident. He glanced at Emily. Funny, but he'd never noticed before how pretty she really was. She smiled at him, showing off a perfect set of sparkling white teeth. Carter returned her smile and then his eyes wandered to Morgan. She wore a white bikini, which contrasted magnificently against her tanned skin. He was overwhelmed by the love he felt for her.

Morgan smiled as she made her way over to him, bent down, and planted a soft kiss on his lips. "Take care of Becca, sweetie. Don't let her wander off."

He squeezed her hand. "Don't worry, honey. She's in good hands. We promise to keep her out of trouble."

Hunter gave Emily a quick hug. "Have fun," he whispered in her ear. "We'll keep the kids here."

"Thanks." Emily smiled weakly, and then joined Morgan, who was already making her way down the path to the lake.

****

"Thanks for giving me a swimming lesson," Emily said.

"No problem." Morgan wasn't in the mood for idle chitchat. She had a lot on her mind and needed to think. She found a secluded spot where large trees and brush obscured them from Carter's and Hunter's hearing and viewing range.

She spread her towel out on the thick grass.

"Nice day," Emily said, stretching her own towel out.

"Yes, it is," Morgan answered lazily. "It's so peaceful here."

"I know. We love it here. We came as much as we could last summer. You should come more often with us." She paused. "I'd really like to get to know you better, Morgan."

Morgan looked at her and smiled. A little late for that, she thought. She gazed at the calm lake. "Well, you game?"

Emily swallowed hard. "I guess it's now or never," she replied uneasily. She sucked in her breath as she looked at the large, formidable lake.

Morgan saw the terror in the woman's eyes. "All right, just watch me. I'm going to swim over to the raft. When I get there, I want you to start wading over. The water's only going to come up to your chest," Morgan explained.

"Up to my chest? Won't it be hard to wade?" Emily shivered.

"You'll be fine. If you have any problem, I'll be right there. Once you reach the raft, we'll go to the other side of it where the water is deeper."

"Isn't the water deep enough here?" Emily asked in a small voice.

"You'll never learn if your feet can touch the bottom."

"Why not? I'd feel more secure. Maybe that's what I should do for the first lesson."

"Suit yourself, but you'll never learn to really swim then if your feet can always touch the bottom."

"I don't know." Emily swallowed hard again. "I don't know if I can even wade that far in such deep water."

"If you don't want to do it, don't worry. We can just go back and join the guys."

"No. I'll do it," she said quickly. "I want to be able to join Hunter on swims. Even the kids swim better than me," she admitted.

"Before you know it you'll be swimming like a pro," Morgan assured her. "Once we get into deeper water you can show me what you can do and we'll take it from there."

"I won't be showing you much," Emily admitted with a frown.

Morgan laughed. "I'm sure you're a better swimmer than you think you are." She slowly waded into the cool water, and then swam gracefully toward the raft.

Emily watched enviously from the shore. Morgan was trying to impress her, and she hated her for that. Truth be told, Emily had disliked Morgan from the moment they were introduced. She had no concrete reason for disliking her. It was one of those things that happened when you first met someone and instantly knew whether you liked that person or didn't. She'd tried to avoid her as much as possible. Hunter liked her, though, and that had at times put a thorn into their otherwise happy marriage. But at least Payton and Rachel believed her when she confided that Morgan had made snide remarks to her when no one else was around since the same thing had happened to them. But in a crowd, Morgan came off as a kindhearted, gentle-spoken woman. It was hard for anyone who hadn't been victim to her barbs to believe she could ever utter a harsh word to anyone. No matter how she felt about Morgan, she loved Carter despite his choice in a wife. And it was for his sake that she tried to keep the peace and opted to stay out of Payton and Rachel's drama with her.

Morgan reached the raft in no time and hoisted herself on top of it. She waved her arms, gesturing for Emily to join her. Emily nervously stepped into the water. She shivered with dread as the cool water inched up her body with every step she took. She felt Morgan's eyes on her, making it feel like an eternity before she finally reached the raft. Morgan reached down and grabbed her arms as Emily awkwardly climbed onto the raft.

"The water's a little chilly still," Morgan said as she dangled her long slender legs over the edge of the raft. "It'll warm up in a couple of weeks."

"I didn't know it was still this cold," Emily answered shivering. She'd love nothing more than to just sit here for an hour and let the warm sun take the chill off.

Morgan turned to her. "Do you and Hunter have much planned for this summer?"

Emily tried to avoid Morgan's penetrating eyes. When she looked at you like she was now looking at Emily, it was like she could read every thought. She shrugged. "Nothing special. We'll probably plan a few day trips…the zoo…some museums…things like that." She gazed out at the calm blue lake, now seeing how calm and beautiful it looked. She wished she felt the same calmness.

Morgan abruptly stood up, and then gracefully dove off the raft and emerged seconds later behind it.

"Come on, try it, Emily," she called. "Dive in."

Emily frowned. "No…I don't know how to dive."

"Come on! You'll never learn if you don't at least try," Morgan said with a touch of disdain in her voice.

"I'll sit on the edge and slide down." She looked at Morgan. "Come closer so I can grab your shoulders."

Morgan rolled her eyes, and then swam over to her. "You'll never learn this way, Emily."

"I need to take baby steps," Emily replied. "I've never gone in a pool or lake where my feet aren't touching the bottom."

"Okay. I'm right here."

Emily tentatively dipped her toes into the water, and then slipped off the raft. She clutched Morgan's shoulders. The sudden weight on Morgan forced her backward, sending both women under water. Emily's head surfaced and she coughed as she reached out feeling the raft. She clung desperately to the side of it. She was scared stiff and yearned to be back on the shore. This was a mistake. She'd never enjoy the water like Morgan did. Carter and the children could swim while she stayed in the shallow end. She didn't care what anyone thought anymore.

Morgan laughed. "Emily, you're supposed to hold your breath. Are you sure you can swim at all?"

"I told you not well." Emily's face heated up from embarrassment. "Look, this was a stupid idea. Let's just forget it." She tried to pull herself back onto the raft. "Can you help me get back up on the raft?"

Morgan said nothing.

"Will you help me?" Emily asked again. She turned her head and looked at Morgan. "Morgan, please, will you help me?"

"Come here," Morgan said quietly.

"No, let's just forget the whole thing," she answered as

she tried to tighten her grip on the raft. Her fingers ached and she was afraid that if she let go she'd sink to the bottom of the lake. "I told you I've changed my mind about the swimming lessons."

"Come here, Emily," Morgan demanded.

Emily turned, startled. Morgan's mouth was twisted into a grotesque smile. Her eyes blazed with loathing. Fear tore through Emily. "I'm…I'm going back, Morgan." Her voice quivered. Before she could move, Morgan was directly behind her. Emily relaxed a little. Good, she's going to help me, she thought. She vowed then and there to never again poke as much as a toe into this lake. She'd be perfectly content to sit on a blanket watching others frolic in the water.

"Don't be afraid, Emily," Morgan whispered. "I've got your back."

"Thank you," Emily whispered.

"Don't thank me yet. You and I need to have a talk."

"We can do it later. Let's get back. The food's probably ready by now."

"It'll wait. Since you don't want to have a chat, I suppose I'll just have to come to the point."

"I don't know what you're talking about, Morgan."

Morgan signed loudly. "It's really a shame that you never thought I was good enough for Carter."

"I don't think that," Emily said quickly. "She didn't like where this conversation was headed.

"Well, at this point it doesn't matter because only one of us will be going back. And I have to tell you, Emily, it won't be you." She laughed. "You brought it on yourself, you know."

"I never did anything to you," Emily whimpered.

"Really?" Morgan asked close to Emily's ear. "You have a very selective memory. But it doesn't matter anymore. I think your time has just run out."

Emily opened her mouth and was ready to scream, but Morgan's hand quickly clamped over it.

"No one will hear you," Morgan said in a low voice. She turned Emily until the woman was facing her.

Emily felt her body began to convulse. A tear slid from her eye. Morgan was sick. Payton and Rachel were right about her. Now she wished she wouldn't have kept silent. But it was too late.

"Do you want to know something funny?" she asked.

Emily's eyes darted back and forth in fear.

Morgan exhaled slowly. "Emily, Emily, you silly little fool. You made this so easy for me. I hadn't quite figured out how to dispose of you and then, bingo! You called and asked me to give you a swimming lesson. What a perfect setup." She grinned. "I must thank you for that," she taunted. "It's a shame that you had an accident."

Emily struggled, but it was useless. Even if she could free herself, Morgan would catch her. She squeezed her eyes shut as the tears slid out. She was going to die and no one would know that it was by Morgan's hand. She thought about her children and Hunter. How she would give anything for just another minute with them. This shouldn't be happening. She was going to be murdered by Carter's wife, but he'd never know that. Everyone would label her death as an accidental drowning. She began to silently pray, but her prayers weren't for herself. They were for protection for Hunter and her children from this monster. Would she target them next?

Morgan pushed her head under water and Emily tried to hold her breath and muster the strength to kick away from her. She had to at least try to save herself. She was bigger than Morgan. If she could overpower her she might have a chance. She reached up and with every ounce of strength left in her body, pulled Morgan's hair dragging her under water.

Taken by surprise, Morgan yelped as her head went under water. She came to the surface sputtering. "You bitch!" she spat out as she grabbed Emily's head tightly and pushed her deeper and deeper under the water.

CHAPTER EIGHT

Justin and Beth rolled a beach ball to Becca. Carter and Hunter sat nearby, laughing at Becca's determination to roll the ball back in a straight line.

"I think the chicken's almost ready," Hunter said.

"I'll check it," Carter said. He stood and then stretched. He walked over to the grill, grabbed the tongs, and picked up a piece. "It looks great!" he said.

"If the girls aren't back in five minutes, I'll go after them." Hunter looked at his wristwatch. "They've been at it for quite a while now."

"I'm just happy to see them finally getting along," Carter admitted.

"You and me both." He pulled himself to his feet.

A piercing scream echoed throughout the lakeside.

Carter dropped the tongs. "What the hell was that?" Hunter asked in a shaky voice.

He looked into his brother's frightened eyes. "It's Morgan! We'd better get down to the lake." He turned to Justin. "Stay here with Becca and Beth, Justin," he ordered.

"Why?" the boy asked.

"Do as your uncle says," Hunter said in a shaky voice. "We'll be right back."

They ran down the path and both stopped dead in their tracks when they saw Morgan hauling a body out of the lake. Seconds later they were at her side panic-stricken.

Hunter dropped to his knees, and then began mouth-to-mouth resuscitation. "Come on, Emily," he cried. "Don't die, honey, please!" He worked feverishly, repeating the steps.

"Carter, I…I tried to get to her, but by the time I did… it was too late," Morgan sobbed.

"We've got to get an ambulance." Carter's knees buckled when he looked at Emily. Hunter turned to him with tears streaming down his face, but Carter already knew what he was going to say before the words came tumbling from his brother's lips.

"She's dead, Carter."

Maybe it was the way Hunter said it, or maybe it was Carter's own fear of death that made his mind momentarily depart from the scene. He watched as though in slow motion as Hunter walked slowly toward Morgan, muttering, "I can't take anymore. We just buried Mom, now Emily's gone." Morgan's screams brought him back to reality.

"You," Hunter said in a strangled voice. "You did this to Emily." His large hands were around her neck.

Carter looked at his wife, as his mind came back to reality. He ran to her and pulled his brother off her. "What the hell are you doing?" he screamed. "Maybe she's still alive. You're not a doctor."

"Look at her," Hunter said hoarsely. "She doesn't have

a pulse."

"Carter," Morgan whimpered as she threw herself into his arms.

Carter held her for a few seconds and then disengaged himself, holding her at arm's length while he studied the marks on her throat. "Are you okay?" he asked in a wobbly voice. If he hadn't been right there, his wife would be dead now, too. His own brother would have committed murder with his bare hands. Hunter's rage toward Morgan alarmed him.

She sniffed as she nodded her head. "I'll be okay."

"We've still got to get an ambulance for Emily," Carter said. He looked at Hunter who'd gone back to Emily and now sat on the ground with her body cradled in his arms. Hunter moaned as he gently rocked her lifeless body back and forth. Carter walked over to him, squatted down, and laid a hand on his brother's shoulder. "Hunter," he said in a quiet voice. "I'm going to get an ambulance and contact Jake. Stay here." He would have sent Morgan but knew she was in no condition to drive.

Hunter nodded but didn't look up.

Carter put an arm around Morgan, drawing her tightly to him. He was scared. First his mother, now his sister-in-law. What was happening? His mind whirled. Two deaths—one accidental, one murder. Why? Why was this happening to his family? Had they had it too good for too long so now they must suffer? He looked into Morgan's beautiful face and then again at her throat.

"What?" she asked quietly.

"Nothing, honey. I was just looking at your neck. I'm

sorry he did that to you. I don't know what came over him."

She squeezed his hand. "It's not your fault, Carter. I know Hunter didn't mean it. He needs to take his hurt and anger out on someone and I suppose I'm the target since I was the last person with Emily."

A million things flowed through Carter's mind as he walked his wife to where the children played. Another funeral had to be planned. The family would have to be contacted, but first Emily's family needed to be notified. How would Hunter raise his children? How would Hunter go on without his wife?

****

Carter dropped Morgan and the children off at his home and called an ambulance and Jake. Before heading back to the lake, he needed to talk to Justin. The boy deserved some answers. Surely, he had to know something tragic had happened to so abruptly cancel their picnic. He hadn't said a word when Carter had instructed him and Beth into the car.

"I need to talk to you, Justin."

"Where's my Mom and Dad, Uncle Carter?" he asked with a stony expression on his face.

Carter looked into the round face, dreading the reaction to his news. He tried to put himself in Justin's place and wondered how he would have reacted to the news he was about to deliver, and at the same time trying to find the right words—words that would somehow soften the blow about the tragedy. "Sit down, Justin." Carter motioned to the sofa.

Justin obediently sat down, but his eyes stayed glued to Carter.

Carter swallowed hard as he kneeled in front of the boy. "Justin, there's been an accident," he said softly. He affectionately put an arm around Justin's shoulder. The boy stiffened and tears brimmed in his eyes.

"Can I see my mom?" he whispered.

Carter swallowed the lump in his throat. "Justin, do you remember what you learned in Sunday school about when God decides he wants someone to come to heaven?"

Justin pulled away. "No!" he shrieked. "God didn't take my mom like he did Gram."

Carter held him close. "I'm sorry, Justin."

The boy shuddered, then squeezed his eyes shut tight for a few seconds. "I don't believe all that stuff about God anymore, then," he said defiantly. "If God loved us then why would he take away my mom, too? It isn't fair!" He pounded his fists into the sofa. "It isn't fair!" he screamed.

"It's okay to cry, Justin," Carter said soothingly, rubbing the boy's back.

Justin looked up at him with blurry eyes. "Men don't cry. Only sissies cry."

"That's not true, Justin. Didn't you cry when Gram died? I did, and you know your father did. We're not sissies."

Justin's lips trembled.

"Grown men cry, Justin. It takes a real man to cry."

Justin's lips quivered as his dam of pain finally burst.

Carter thought his own heart would burst as he held the boy and listened to his heart-wrenching sobs.

****

Back at the lake, Carter pulled up next to the ambulance. Jake Birch and his deputies were talking to Hunter. He hurried

102

over to the group. "The kids are fine, Hunter."

Hunter looked at him through red, swollen eyes. "Thanks," he sniffed. "Who's watching them? The next-door neighbor? She was one of Emily's best friends."

"No, Morgan is taking care of them for now."

Hunter's jaw dropped. "No! I don't want her near my kids. She killed my wife."

"Was Morgan with Emily at the time of her drowning?" Jake asked.

"She – she killed my wife!" Hunter choked.

Jake frowned. "Did either of you witness the drowning?" Jake asked.

"No. We were with the kids. Grilling the food," Carter explained.

"Morgan was alone with her. She did it," Hunter insisted.

"Hunter, you know that's nonsense. You're just upset and want to blame someone." Carter turned to Jake. "He doesn't know what he's saying." He glanced over at the medical examiner who was finishing his examination of Emily's corpse. "It was an accidental drowning, Jake. Emily was a poor swimmer," Carter explained.

Jake looked at Hunter, who had walked over to where his wife's body was being put on a stretcher. He stood quietly gazing down on her. Within a few weeks, two members from the same family were dead. Something was wrong, terribly wrong. "Carter, where's Morgan? I need to question her."

"I took her and the kids home. She's taking this extremely hard, Jake, and I don't think she should be questioned right now. Can't it wait for a day or so? After all, this was an accident."

Jake frowned. "I need to question her as soon as possible, Carter. Since she was with Emily when Emily drowned, I have a few questions that need answers." He looked at his deputies. They were both young, strong men in their late twenties. James Wylmer had been with him for five years, Jason Tismont for three. They were local boys and two of the best as far as Jake could see.

"Jason, ask Tom to come here when he's finished," Jake instructed Tismont. Something about what Hunter had said about Morgan Rogers disturbed him. Sweat trickled down his back. Something was happening to his peaceful town and he didn't like it. He didn't like it at all, but he didn't know how he could prevent it either. He tensed.

The medical examiner, Tom Hannigan, slowly made his way over to Jake. Jake noticed how old Tom was getting. His shoulders were stooped and his steel gray hair glistened in the sun's sharp rays. "What'd you find, Tom?"

Tom pulled on his chin. "Well, Jake," he began, "she drowned all right, no doubt about that, but..." He gave Carter a sharp look.

"But what?" Jake asked impatiently. "Was there anything unusual?"

"There are some marks on her body."

"What kind of marks?" Jake demanded.

"Scratches."

"Do you have any idea what could have caused them?"

"Not without an autopsy."

"All right, Tom, then let me know when you have the results," Jake said.

Jake turned his attention back to Carter. "Tell your wife I'll be by about seven to question her."

"Let her rest tonight, Jake. She's been through a trauma."

"I need to question her while the events are fresh in her mind."

Carter's eyes narrowed. "Jake, you can't possibly believe Morgan had anything to do with Emily's death."

"Carter, I'm certainly not accusing her of anything." He looked into Carter's eyes. "Why are you so defensive? My questioning of her is standard practice." He paused. "But before you arrived, Hunter informed me that the wives didn't associate frequently and actually had some animosity between them."

"They may not have gotten along well in the past, but they were mending fences," Carter stated emphatically. "And may I add, Emily called and asked her to join us at the lake today and also asked if Morgan would give her a swimming lesson. Hunter doesn't know what he's saying. My God, Jake, please give us some time to grieve in peace!"

"Tell Morgan I'll be by this evening."

CHAPTER NINE

Morgan hurried upstairs and slipped out of her damp swimsuit. She quickly threw on a pair of too-tight jeans and a blouse. She grabbed the small steel box from under the nightstand table, then unlocked it and removed the paper. Next to Emily's name, she wrote: "Completed June 5, 1983." She marveled at her luck in having this opportunity placed in her lap. She hadn't figured out the means of Emily's demise until the swimming lesson afforded her the singular opportunity. She thought Emily would be one of the last to go, but it was much better this way. It was easy and would be ruled an accidental death with no investigators snooping around.

She put the box away, and then walked downstairs. She watched from the entrance of the living room as Justin poured out his grief in long, shuddering sobs. His sister sat nearby. The look of fear on her face proved to Morgan that Beth did not comprehend what was going on. She debated going to her and her brother and trying to offer some comfort, and then decided against it. She couldn't stand them. They were young and would get over it. Before summer ended,

106

their mother would probably be just a fond memory that would fade with time.

She entered the kitchen, where she encountered Becca sitting in the middle of the floor, pots and pans strewn about her. Morgan laughed as she spread some jam on a slice of bread, and then handed it to her daughter. Becca impishly smiled up at her as she bit into the treat, smearing jelly on her face. Morgan laughed again as she bent to kiss the top of her daughter's head.

****

Jake Birch drove to the Fairview Hotel where Mark Barlow had taken residence ever since he had arrived in town. He wanted to fill him in on Emily Rogers' death. Even though he knew the drowning of Emily Rogers would be viewed by almost everyone as accidental, something about the circumstances of her drowning didn't sit right with him. Something was off. He felt it in his gut. Normally he wouldn't have felt the need to inform the investigator, but since Emily was the daughter-in-law of the victim in their murder investigation, he felt Barlow had the right to know.

He impatiently knocked on Barlow's door. The door was opened almost immediately as though Barlow was getting ready to leave.

Barlow looked surprised to see him. "Come in, Sheriff," he said, moving slightly so Jake could push past him. "What brings you here?"

"I've got some news you might be interested in." Jake glanced around the room. Not bad, he thought. It sported a small kitchenette complete with a table and two chairs, and a comfortable sitting area with a loveseat and an easy chair. He assumed that the two closed doors contained the bathroom and a bedroom.

Mark motioned to the loveseat. "Please have a seat. Can I get you some coffee?"

"Yes, black, please," Jake replied. "If it's no bother."

"No bother," Mark replied. He poured two cups of coffee and then handed one to Jake. After Jake was seated on the loveseat, Mark took the easy chair. "What's the information?" he finally asked.

"Emily Rogers had an accident this afternoon. She's dead." He waited for Barlow's reaction.

Mark raised his eyebrows. "What happened?"

"A drowning," Jake stated.

Mark studied him. "And you don't believe she drowned?"

Jake exhaled loudly. "At this point I don't know what I believe." He shook his head. "Something doesn't feel right about it."

"How is Emily related?"

"She's married to Hunter Rogers."

Mark leaned forward, intrigued. "Fill me in."

"Her sister-in-law, Morgan Rogers, was giving her a swimming lesson when Emily apparently drowned."

"Hmm...any witnesses?" Mark asked.

"No, Morgan was the only one there."

"Who recovered the body?" He took a gulp of his coffee as he waited for the sheriff's answer.

"Morgan pulled Emily out of the water. Hunter tried to revive her to no avail."

Mark eyed Jake thoughtfully. "Did you question

Hunter?"

"Yes," Jake answered, shifting in the seat. "He's accused Morgan of causing his wife's death."

"What has Morgan stated about the alleged accident?"

"I haven't questioned her yet. I'm going over about seven tonight."

Barlow's eyes narrowed. "What makes you suspicious?"

Jake looked at the younger man. "Tom Hannigan, the medical examiner, found scratches on Emily's body."

"Does he believe them to be suspicious?"

"He's conducting an autopsy."

"I can understand your suspicions. It could be that Emily Rogers drowned with just a little bit of help." He took another sip of coffee. "How did Carter Rogers react to his brother's accusation against his wife?"

"He became upset and objected to my questioning her tonight."

"Maybe I should come with you," Mark said.

"I thought you might want to," Jake replied.

****

Carter pulled up into his driveway with Hunter, in his car, behind him. He got out of his car, walked to Hunter's, and peered into the driver's side window. "Hunter, are you sure you don't want to stay with us for a while? I don't think you should be alone."

Hunter shook his head as he kept his hands on the steering wheel. "No, I need to be home. The kids will feel better in their own home." His voice was cold.

"Listen, Hunter," Carter said, laying a hand on his brother's shoulder. "I know how you must be feeling right now, but—"

"No, you don't!" Hunter said sharply. "No one knows how I'm feeling! How could you? You haven't lost your wife…your whole world hasn't just fallen apart!"

"Hunter, let me at least contact Emily's family for you…and ours."

He nodded as he ran a hand through his hair. "Thanks for telling Justin and Beth. I'll have a long talk with them."

Carter sighed. "Hunter, you know deep down in your heart that Morgan had nothing to do with Emily's drowning. You have to know it was just a horrible accident."

Hunter glared at him. "You'll never convince me that she didn't murder my wife," he hissed. "No one will ever convince me otherwise."

"Let's sit down like rational adults and let Morgan explain to you what really happened."

He threw his hands up. "Why, Carter? What is it going to take to convince you that your wife is not the sweet, loving woman you think she is?" He shook his head. "Why can't you see it, Carter?" His voice cracked. "Emily told me how Morgan treated her when no one was around to witness it. It's the same thing Mom used to say. I told Emily to just ignore her. So Emily sucked it up just to keep peace. Asking Morgan for a swimming lesson was her way to try to get to know her and settle whatever it was that Morgan seemed to have against her." He cleared his throat. "And that was a big step for Emily since you're well aware that she's never been comfortable in the water. Drowning was her biggest fear. Did Morgan know that?"

Carter's jaw tightened. "Hunter, you're talking crazy. I

don't think you even know what you're saying."

Hunter looked squarely at him. "She has you brainwashed, Carter. I hope to hell you wake up before it's too late."

Carter rolled his eyes. "Don't be ridiculous."

"I'm serious," he answered in a calmer voice. "What is it, Carter? She can't be that good in bed. Or is she? Is that why you married her so quickly? After all, she's much younger than you."

"You're losing your mind," Carter said, anger beginning to once again arise in him. He had to remind himself that his brother was only talking this way because of his grief and later would regret what he'd said. He inhaled deeply. Now wasn't the time to get into an argument. He put his anger under control. "Let's just drop it, Hunter."

Hunter nodded. "Please send out Justin and Beth." He looked in the car mirror. "You might as well take the food."

"The kids might want it later," Carter answered.

"No," he said firmly. "It'll just be an unpleasant reminder of what happened today." He gripped the steering wheel.

Carter opened the backseat car door and removed the coolers containing the food. "Call if you need anything, Hunter."

"We'll be fine."

"Okay, then. I'll send the kids right out," he said. He glanced back at the car. Hunter sat stony-faced watching him.

****

"Hi, honey," Carter said walking into the family room where Morgan sat in a rocking chair with Becca. "How are

Justin and Beth doing?"

"As well as can be expected. They haven't said much and I couldn't get them to eat a bite." Her eyes clouded. "Those poor kids. I wish there was some way I could comfort them, but neither of them will even talk to me. They've been sitting in front of the TV like statues."

"It's not you, honey. They've had a terrible shock. It'll take time for them to be back to normal." He walked over to Beth and Justin. "Your father's waiting in the car for you two," he said softly.

Justin looked at him and then grabbed his sister's hand. "Come on, Beth."

Carter watched as they slowly got into the car. He waited until Hunter pulled out of the driveway, and then walked back into the family room. He sat on the sofa. "What a day," he said. "I can't believe Emily's really gone. This is surreal."

"There's no guarantees in life, Carter. Everyone goes through tragedy." Morgan's eyes were focused on her slumbering daughter.

Carter thought her reply odd, but quickly dismissed it. "Jake Birch wants to question you about the drowning. He's coming over about seven."

She shrugged her shoulders. "I suppose that's routine," she calmly answered as she raised her eyes to him.

"I'll put Becca to bed if you want to freshen up before he gets here."

"Okay," she said, shifting so he could pick up Becca.

"Does your neck hurt?" he asked tenderly.

She nodded. "I'll survive."

"I'm sorry Hunter did that to you. I know he didn't mean it."

She looked hard at her husband. "I think he did."

****

Carter tucked his daughter in, and then tiptoed out of her room. He walked into the master bedroom and sat on the edge of the bed, then rested his face in his hands dreading the phone calls he had to make. He was emotionally drained, but he had to gather every ounce of strength he could to help his brother as well as offer support to his wife. He thought Hunter was losing his mind with his unfounded accusations against Morgan, and he was hurt with Hunter's damning remarks, but his brother was hurting far worse than he was. *At least I still have my wife,* he thought. He couldn't imagine how he would feel at this exact moment if it had been Morgan who drowned instead of Emily. A shudder tore through him. Still, he was upset that Hunter had physically harmed his wife and if it hadn't been under such horrific circumstances, he would have ripped him apart.

With sweaty palms, he picked up the cordless phone. He flipped through the address book until he found Emily's parents' phone number. He steeled himself and then quickly punched in the numbers.

"Hello," a pleasant voice greeted him.

"Mrs. Henderson?"

"Yes, who is this?"

"This is Hunter's brother Carter." He heard the slight hesitation as though the woman's air supply had been cut off. "Mrs. Henderson?"

"I'm here. What's happened?" she asked quickly. "It's

113

bad news, isn't it, Carter? You wouldn't be calling otherwise."

Carter noted how quickly her voice had become high-pitched. He wished he could find the words to soften the blow he was about to deliver. "I'm afraid so. There's been an accident."

"Oh my God, Bill!" she screamed.

Carter wiped his hands on his pants as he listened to Emily's mother screaming for her husband. Seconds later Emily's father's panic-stricken voice came over the line.

"Carter, this is Bill Henderson," he said in a shaky voice. "My wife says there's been an accident."

"I'm sorry to have to tell you this, Mr. Henderson, but Emily drowned this afternoon."

"No!" the man moaned. "How?"

"It was during a swimming lesson."

"Swimming lesson? She hates the water. Please give me the details." He sniffed.

Carter painfully relayed the afternoon's events for Emily's father, his own heart breaking as he listened to the man's mournful sobs. "I'm so sorry," was all he could manage to say.

"How are Hunter and the children holding up?" Bill asked, after he'd gained some control.

Carter squeezed his eyes tightly shut. "Not well, Mr. Henderson...that's why I'm calling you instead of Hunter. I'm staying close to him. I'll see if he's up to calling you later."

"Carter, please be with him and the children until we can get there. I'll get the first flight out."

"I promise," Carter replied.

He set the phone down, and then rubbed his eyes. He

dreaded the rest of the calls he had to make, but they were inevitable. He picked the phone back up and quickly dialed Raine's number. "Hi, Raine, this is Carter. I'm afraid I have some bad news."

"What, Carter?" she asked fearfully.

He hesitated, and then decided he might as well just come right out with it. "It's Emily. She drowned at the lake this afternoon."

"No, Carter. This can't be happening. Who's targeting our family?"

"It was an accident, Raine," Carter said patiently. "Accidents do happen." He instantly regretted his last remark the moment the words were out of his mouth. "I'm sorry, Raine. I don't mean to make light of it. It's been one hell of a day."

"I can't believe Emily's gone," Raine said in a trembling voice. "Have Emily's parents been notified? Aren't they out of town?"

"Yes, they're on vacation in North Carolina. I just got off the phone with them. They're getting a flight back as soon as they can."

"I'll get home as soon as I can, too. Hunter must be falling apart. Is he with you and Morgan, I hope?"

"He's in pretty bad shape, Raine." He decided not to tell her about Hunter's attack on Morgan. "He refused to stay. He wants to be in his own home with the kids."

"I guess I get that." She drew a shuddering breath. "You said Emily drowned? How could that happen? She's never gone in water deeper than her knees. Was she on a boat or something? Did she fall overboard?"

"No, she decided she wanted to learn to swim and went in the deep part of the lake near the raft."

"That doesn't make sense."

"I don't know, Raine," he said wearily. "I've got more calls to make." He paused. "Could you break the news to Payton for me? I have to call the rest of the family." Payton would be inconsolable, hence his decision to have Raine break the catastrophic news to her. He was in no condition to defend his wife to his sister, as Payton would force him to do.

"Of course, Carter. I'll take a taxi to her place as soon as I get off the phone," she answered. "I know Payton's going to have questions. Was anyone with Emily when she drowned? I can't imagine she just went into the lake and waded over to the raft. Do you know how it happened?"

Carter slowly let his breath out. He had to give her an explanation. "Hunter and Emily invited us to the lake for a barbeque. Emily asked Morgan if she would teach her to swim."

"I see," Raine replied quietly. "Did you see it happen?"

"No, Morgan said that Emily apparently went under and didn't resurface. By the time Morgan got to her it was too late."

"It still doesn't make sense that she'd be by the raft."

"I could have the details wrong. I know Morgan was at the raft. Maybe Emily wanted to impress her." He cleared his throat. "I'm sure by the time you get here we'll have the facts of how it happened. Morgan's pretty shaken up over it." He knew she wasn't as shaken up as he'd thought she should be, but then surmised that Hunter's anger toward her had caused her to emotionally close up. That was the only logical explanation he could come up with. Hopefully by the time everyone arrived, Hunter would realize that his accusations against Morgan were unfounded.

"I can only imagine what Morgan's going through. How are you coping, Carter?"

"As best as I can." He rubbed his jaw. "Let me know when you'll be here."

"I will," she promised.

He clicked off the phone, and then reached for his address book once again. The next hour was emotionally draining as he relayed the horrific news to the rest of his family.

Paul's voice trembled as he pleaded with Carter to give him a blow-by-blow description of the day's events leading up to Emily's death. Carter calmly and patiently relived the day. By now it was becoming almost automatic, as though he wasn't really there, but listening to someone else retelling the events. His final call was to Collin and Jude. They both received the news calmly, unlike Sarah and Paul. When he finished, he walked back downstairs. He was restless. He needed to do something physical.

"I'm going to ride up to the lake."

"Now?" Morgan asked surprised. "You won't be here when the sheriff arrives?"

"I'll be back in plenty of time."

Her eyes narrowed. "Why do you want to go back there after what happened?"

Carter shoved his hands in his pockets. "I don't know," he replied.

He walked to the garage and retrieved his ten-speed

bike. A half hour later he arrived at the lake. Hardly anyone came here anymore, unlike past years when it was a popular spot for families. The last few times he'd been here, including today, they were the only family around. He hadn't minded, in fact, he loved the seclusion. He parked his bike and then walked down to the water's edge. The lake was as much a part of his boyhood as the family home had been. His family had spent many lazy hours here in the summer picnicking. This had always been a special place to him. Now an ugly event marred it forever. It would never be the same, it couldn't be. The peace it once held for him now only bore a hideous reminder of what had taken place. There were no new memories to be made here. This would be the last time he'd ever come here. He took one last look, his heart heavy with grief and loss.

When he arrived home, he found Morgan still in the family room, lying on the sofa. He quietly walked over to her and knelt beside her. "Are you sure you're all right, honey?" he tenderly asked as he lightly ran his fingertips down her arm. "Maybe we should have you checked out."

She smiled. "No, I'm fine. I'm just not looking forward to talking to Sheriff Birch. I get the impression he doesn't like me." She puckered. "I don't know why."

Carter sighed. "Jake's hard to figure out sometimes, honey. Believe me, it has nothing to do with you. He's never taken to outsiders moving into town." He ran his fingertips through her hair. "Don't worry about Jake. Tell him exactly what happened today. I know it won't be easy to go through it again, but you have to."

She nodded just as the doorbell sounded.

"I suppose that's him."

"I'll get it," Carter said as he headed toward the door.

He pulled open the door surprised to see that Jake had brought someone with him. "Please come in," Carter offered. Jake Birch and Mark Barlow followed him into the family room where Morgan was sitting calmly waiting for them.

"Evening, Mrs. Rogers," Jake said politely.

"Please call me Morgan," she replied with a forced smile.

Jake motioned to his companion. "I'd like you both to meet Mark Barlow." He looked at Carter. "Mr. Barlow's working on your mother's case," he explained.

"Any suspects?" Carter questioned, eyeing the investigator.

"Nothing concrete," Mark replied.

"In other words nothing," Carter said tartly.

"I have some questions for you about what happened at the lake this afternoon, Morgan," Jake said, ignoring Carter.

Carter figured as much. It was going to end up a cold case, but Jake wouldn't tell him that. He watched the men seat themselves after Morgan offered them to do so. He didn't like the way they were looking at his wife. He wondered what was going through Morgan's mind. He could read nothing in her eyes.

Morgan nodded. "Of course."

"Am I correct in assuming you were the only person with Emily Rogers at the time of her drowning?" Jake asked peering closely at her.

"That's right." She drew a calming breath. He was staring intently at her. She was vulnerable as though the clothes had been torn from her body leaving her naked and exposed. She had to keep her cool even though it was making her uneasy with his probing eyes. "Would anyone care for some coffee or a soda?" she offered.

"No, thank you," Jake answered.

She slightly turned her head and looked at Mark Barlow who had seated himself next to her on the sofa. Jake and Carter sat in the two easy chairs facing the sofa. A large coffee table separated them.

"You and Emily decided to take a swim together?" Jake asked.

"Not exactly. Emily asked me to give her a swimming lesson. I had no idea she was such a poor swimmer." She blinked hard as her eyes brimmed with tears. "She dove off the raft and when she didn't resurface, I dove in after her, but I couldn't find her right away. By the time I did, it was too late." She shuddered and swallowed hard.

Jake frowned. "Why would a poor swimmer dive off a raft in the deepest part of the lake?"

Morgan shrugged. "I don't know. Maybe she didn't want me to know she was as bad a swimmer as she was." She threw her hands up. "How would I know why she did it?"

Jake hastily wrote down her account of the accident. Mark Barlow still kept his eyes glued to her face and then focused on her bruised neck. "What happened to your neck?" he asked.

Morgan stole a glance at Carter. He nodded. "I... Hunter did it," she said flatly. "He was justifiably upset and lashed out," she explained quickly. Her hand trembled as she pushed her hair back from her brow. Mark's eyes moved to her hands and it unnerved her.

Jake eyed her suspiciously. "Did you push Emily Rogers off the raft?" he asked abruptly catching her off guard.

Her eyes widened. "No!" she exclaimed, jumping up from the sofa. She ran to Carter, who was already on his feet. He put his arms protectively around her.

"That's enough, Jake!" Carter bellowed. "How dare you!"

"There are scratch marks, like the kind from long fingernails, on Emily Rogers' neck," he explained as his eyes traveled to Morgan's fingernails.

"If there are scratch marks anywhere on Emily's body then I must've scratched her when I was pulling her in!" Morgan cried. "That's the only way she could have gotten any scratches."

"I think you and Mr. Barlow had better leave, Jake!" Carter insisted. "Unless you plan to charge my wife for an accident!

"I'm only doing my job," Jake insisted, eyeing Morgan cautiously. "I'll call you if I have any further questions."

CHAPTER TEN

"What do you think?" Jake asked Barlow after they were back in the sheriff's office.

"Morgan Rogers is lying," Mark stated as he leaned back in a chair.

"I got the same impression. I don't think Emily Rogers drowned. Not accidentally, anyway."

"Unfortunately," Barlow said, "we don't have any sound evidence against her." He frowned. "We've got to catch her off guard."

"How do we do that?" Jake stared intently at him.

"We're going to have to keep very close tabs on her every move. But we'll have to be careful not to let her know. We have to convince her that we don't suspect her of foul play. If she finds out, the consequences could be disastrous."

Jake lifted an eyebrow. "Disastrous how?"

Mark was thoughtful for a moment. "I worked on a case like this about ten years ago."

"What happened?" Jake asked.

He exhaled slowly. "A young woman did away with her entire family, one member at a time, over a period of five years.

She was good, very good, and no one suspected anything to be amiss. She was living the perfect life." He laughed sourly. "Her neighbors and friends even gave her glowing character references. In fact, she was the neighborhood babysitter."

"How was she caught?"

"When she had murdered the final member of her family, her mind snapped, just like that." He snapped a pencil in two for emphasis.

Jake straightened. "Do you think Morgan Rogers fits that type of profile?"

"I honestly don't know." He stood up. "What I do know is that she's lying. I feel it in the pit of my stomach."

****

Carter rubbed Morgan's back. "Don't worry, sweetie," he said soothingly. "Nobody's going to believe you had anything to do with Emily's death. It's a ridiculous notion."

"But, Carter, do you realize what Sheriff Birch's accusations could do to my reputation?" she raged. "There should be a law against this type of badgering! Maybe we should talk to a lawyer."

"If we go to a lawyer, then it will look like we have something to hide." Her muscles were tight. "Calm down," he whispered against her ear. "It won't do either of us any good to dwell on it."

"I can't let it go, Carter. I haven't hurt anyone." She gritted her teeth.

"I know you haven't, honey," he said softly. "I promise you that no one will ever hurt you." He stroked her hair as she rested her head against him.

"I wish I could believe that. I'm sorry I ever came to this

damned town. We should have moved somewhere away from your family."

Carter's jaw tightened. "We hardly see them. They haven't bothered us."

"You don't see how they treat me behind your back when we do get together with them." Her eyes blazed.

"I thought we put that all behind us and you wanted to make a fresh start. I think we should cancel our plans to visit Payton, Paul, and Sarah."

She shook her head. "No, you're right. I do want a fresh start with them." She exhaled loudly. "If Emily wouldn't have died maybe she and I could have even gotten along eventually."

Carter's brow creased as he thought about what she'd just said, but he didn't respond.

****

Later Carter sat at his kitchen table, munching on some popcorn. He opened a can of beer and took a long swallow. Something wasn't right, but he couldn't quite put his finger on it. He'd defend his wife at any cost, but her story to Jake Birch and Mark Barlow didn't coincide with what she said earlier to him. He knew he should've questioned her about it, but she was under enough stress. He'd do it when things calmed down. As for her practically being accused of drowning Emily, the idea was ludicrous. She and Emily were never friends, but that didn't make her a murderer. He was frustrated that no one ever took the time to see the side of her he knew and loved, the side that was kind, patient, and gentle. She devoted herself to making him and Becca happy.

He finished his beer, turned out the kitchen light, and

then walked back into the family room. Morgan was sound asleep on the sofa. He didn't have the heart to wake her. She looked peaceful and he was relieved that she was getting some much needed rest after the ordeal she'd been through. He grabbed the quilt from the back of the sofa and carefully placed it over her, then softly kissed her forehead.

****

Morgan stirred. A pounding echoed in her ears. She tried to focus on it. It seemed to be coming from a distance. It persisted. She rolled onto her side, and then opened her sleep-heavy eyes. The pounding grew closer, more insistent and louder. She sat up and rubbed the sleep from her eyes. She looked around herself realizing she was still on the sofa in the family room where she'd fallen asleep earlier. She was surprised that Carter had left her to sleep on the sofa — alone — all night. Her heart sank for a moment. The pounding stopped. She was grateful until the chiming of the doorbell startled her. She sat listening, hoping it would stop. When it didn't, she reluctantly got up and went to the door. She opened it.

Hunter glared coldly at her from the other side. "Where's Carter?" he demanded.

"I suppose he's asleep," she answered stifling a yawn.

"Get him!"

The tone of his voice jolted her awake. "Listen, Hunter, I won't have you coming to my home and talking to me this way. Where are your kids anyway?"

Hunter ignored her. "If you won't get him then I'll get him myself!" He pushed past her and stomped to the stairs. "Carter! Carter!" he shouted.

"Stop it, Hunter," Morgan ordered. "You'll wake Becca."

He glared at her. "Tough! Carter!" His voice grew louder.

Morgan grabbed his arm. "Get out of my house this instant!" she hissed. "If you don't you'll be sorry!" she warned.

"Do you think you're going to throw me out of my brother's house?" he taunted as he stood smirking down at her, feet slightly apart.

Morgan's eyes softened. "I always liked you, Hunter. Why are you treating me this way? What have I ever done to you?"

His shook his head in wonder as he glared at her. "Let me refresh your memory," he said, pointing a finger at her. "You murdered my wife! And if it's the last thing I do, I'm going to prove it!"

"No, Hunter, I didn't. I told you what happened." She looked at him sympathetically.

"I didn't buy your story then and I certainly don't now!"

"Don't you know how terrible I feel knowing I couldn't reach Emily in time? This hasn't been easy for me, Hunter."

"Don't try to pacify me, you stupid bitch! Your only purpose in life is self-gratification!" He trembled. "You'd better thank your lucky stars that Carter prevented me from strangling you yesterday!" he screamed. "I wanted to choke the life right out of you just like you did to Emily!"

Carter appeared at the top of the stairs. "What the hell is going on?" he demanded as he looked at Hunter and then Morgan.

Morgan shrugged. "Hunter came by to see you. I'll put some coffee on," she said as she walked out of the room.

"What's wrong, Hunter? It's only six o'clock!" Carter hurried downstairs.

"I know what time it is, Carter. I'm sorry I woke you." He stood unsteadily. "I just had to get out of the house."

"It's okay," Carter quickly reassured him. He looked into his brother's red-rimmed eyes. The eyes that had always been bright and clear were now dull and looking old. The light had vanished from them. Hunter's forehead was creased with deep lines. For the first time, Carter saw the toll their mother's and now Hunter's wife's deaths had taken on him. "Where are the kids?"

"Home. Emily's parents arrived late last night. We're going to make the funeral — " His voice broke.

Hunter threw his arms around him. "Is there anything I can do for you, Hunter?"

He cleared his throat. "No. I'll let you know when we have the arrangements made."

"How are Emily's parents holding up?"

"Not well. We had to get her mother a sedative to calm her down." He held onto Carter's arm. "I don't know if I can get through this, Carter." Tears spilled from his eyes and he swiped at them with the back of his hand. "I know I have to keep it together for the kids' sakes."

Carter was at a loss for words. He knew that nothing anyone could say would help to relieve any of the pain his brother was experiencing.

"Why don't you sit down and have a cup of coffee?"

"I don't think I could handle another cup." He

hesitated. "I'm thinking about leaving Weldon. Emily and I were discussing a job offer I received. Even though it pays almost double what I'm making now, we'd decided to turn it down since Emily didn't want to leave Weldon and her family, but now I don't think I can stay." He swallowed hard. "I haven't made a concrete decision yet."

Carter was momentarily stunned with his news. There would be no one except him left in Weldon. He had to put his own feelings aside and concentrate on his brother. "I'll miss you if you go, Hunter."

He flashed a weak smile. "It's not like we've spent much time together in the past few years. Not like we used to before...well, you know what I mean."

Carter did know what he meant, but now was not the time to get into an argument about Morgan so instead he just nodded. He turned his head when he heard someone coming.

Morgan walked up to him, carrying a tray filled with coffee and donuts. "Coffee?" she offered. "I thought we could have it in the living room."

"Sure, honey," Carter answered.

"Hunter, would you like a cup?" she asked.

Hunter turned toward her. "I don't want anything from you," he said icily, then turned his attention back to Carter. "I have to get going. I'll let you know about the arrangements."

"I'll call you later."

He nodded and then walked to the door.

Carter followed him and placed a hand on his arm. "Hunter, I'm truly sorry, but please don't blame any of this on Morgan. It was an accident. If it had been the other way around, I wouldn't have blamed Emily."

Hunter gave Carter a hard look. "I wish it had been the other way around." His voice was hard. "For all our sakes, I wish it had been the other way around." He slammed the door on his way out.

Morgan poured two cups of coffee. She handed Carter a cup. "Honey, I know Hunter's upset, but I'm tired of him blaming me for the drowning."

He sighed. "I know." He patted her arm.

"When's the funeral?"

"He'll let me know later."

She sipped her coffee. "I don't think I should go."

He studied her. "I don't think you should either."

****

Jake Birch walked slowly through the business district of Weldon. The city was beginning to stir. This was his favorite time of the day. He liked the peacefulness of the early morning, before the streets became clogged with cars and people hurrying every which way. He stopped for a moment to look at a window display of men's casual summer wear and was reminded of his scanty wardrobe. He walked past a few more storefronts, and then entered Nora's Cafe.

"'Morning, Jake," Nora cheerfully greeted him.

"Good morning, Nora. I'll have a cup of coffee and a jelly donut." He perched his heavy body on a stool at the counter.

Nora brought the coffee and donut. "It was a real shame about Emily Rogers' drowning." She leaned an elbow on the counter. "Such a nice woman. And those poor little kids," she said sympathetically.

"Yeah, it sure was." Jake bit into his donut. Nora picked

129

up a cloth and wiped the counter.

Jake watched her as she worked. He'd known Nora for most of his life. They'd been in the same classes all through school. She married a boy from Norwood when she was eighteen, but two years later, her husband ran off with her best friend, leaving her shattered. She'd never heard from either since. After a few years, she filed for divorce. She never remarried even though she'd had her fair share of proposals, Jake being one of them. They'd dated off and on over the years, but their relationship never developed into anything more than a deep friendship even though Jake had wanted more.

"Two deaths in the family in such a short amount of time. Any leads in Rachel Rogers' murder case?" she asked.

"Nothing yet, Nora, but, I'm working on a few hunches."

"Like what?" She leaned closer to him with her eyebrows raised.

"You know I can't tell you official business." He laughed.

Nora laughed, too. "Thought I could trip you up."

"It'll never happen," he said with a wink.

"Well, you can't blame a girl for trying." She refilled his cup. "No more prying. I promise."

"What's new with you, Nora?" he asked.

"Oh, nothing earth-shattering. You remember my youngest sister Jane?" she asked.

He nodded.

"She's coming for a visit next month."

"Oh good! I'll have to stop by to say hello."

"She's bringing her three teenagers with her." Nora rolled her eyes. "I love them to death, but last year they almost drove me out of my mind with their loud music and everything else teens do." She smiled.

"You know you loved every minute of it, noise and all," he said.

She looked sheepishly at him. "I really did. After they left, it was hard to get used to the house being so quiet."

"Where's Jane living now? They've moved around quite a bit."

"Texas."

"How's her husband Joe?"

"He just got a big promotion, but it looks like he won't be transferred this time. I'm happy for them because they really love Texas. I went there last year for a visit and they're trying to get me out there again this fall."

"I remember when you went. This place wasn't the same without you here." He grinned at her and watched a slight blush color her cheeks. He knew it was no secret to her that his feelings for her still had much deeper roots than just friendship. "Even though I'd miss you, it would do you good to get away once in a while," he said.

"I know," she agreed. "I'm not getting any younger, so I suppose I should quit putting everything off until tomorrow. Someday I'm going to wake up to find out it's already tomorrow." She grinned.

Jake looked at her beautiful, flawless skin as she talked. To him she had never aged. She could still pass for forty. Her chestnut hair didn't have a trace of gray in it. "I'll have one more cup of coffee, Nora," he said. "Then I have to get back to work."

She refilled his cup. "I'm giving a small dinner party next week, Jake. I'd like you to come."

He pulled on his chin. "I don't know, Nora, but thanks for the invitation." As much as he'd give his eyeteeth to spend some time with Nora, he didn't care much for formal dinner parties.

"Come on," she prodded. "It'll be fun."

"Who'll be there?" he asked tentatively.

"Just a few mutual friends. No one you don't know." She patted his arm. "You don't even have to get dressed up. It's very casual. Besides, I'm doing all the cooking."

He peered into her eyes. "You got me. You know I can't resist your cooking."

She laughed. "I'll phone you later with the details."

He watched as she hurried over to a customer. He finished his coffee, and then laid a few bills on the counter.

He walked back to his office. He sat at his desk and went over his notes on Emily Rogers' drowning. He studied the answers Morgan Rogers had given to the questions he'd asked. How could he prove she had something to do with the drowning? There was something about her that rubbed him the wrong way. He didn't like her. From the moment he'd met her he sensed something was off where she was concerned. She was friendly enough, but standoffish at the same time. No one really knew her or anything about her past. Mark Barlow had been right when he cautioned to keep an eye on her.

****

Jude loaded the dishwasher, and then pressed the start button. Collin poured himself a cup of coffee and stirred some

132

cream into it. "I'm not looking forward to another funeral," he said as he seated himself on a stool and leaned his elbows on the counter.

"Me either. It seems like we just got back from your mom's."

He stared into his cup. "Hunter's got to be going through hell." He sighed. "Life certainly can throw you some curves." He buttered a piece of toast.

"I know. We can't take anything for granted."

"Where are the kids?" Collin asked.

"Still in bed. Remember you gave them permission to stay up and watch a late movie on TV last night?" She looked quizzically at him.

He rubbed his temples. "I forgot. It doesn't hurt them to stay up late once in a while, I suppose. But we have to be careful not to make a habit out of it."

"I wonder how Morgan's coping with Emily's death," Jude said. "She's got to be beside herself knowing she couldn't save her."

"I wonder," Collin replied.

****

Raine turned when Payton entered the kitchen. "I just put the coffee on. Would you like me to fix you some breakfast, Payton?" she offered. She'd spent the night because of Payton's reaction to the news. She couldn't leave her alone. Payton had gone to pieces and her reaction alarmed Raine.

"No. I don't want anything," Payton replied. "Dammit, Raine, I'll bet my life Emily didn't drown without some help!"

Raine raised her eyebrows in surprise. "What are you

talking about?" She looked skeptically at her sister.

"Morgan murdered Emily," Payton stated.

"Payton! That's a horrible thing to say!" Raine was shocked that her sister could even conjure up such a ridiculous notion.

Payton blinked. "I know she did it. Mark my words, Raine. Someday you'll figure it out for yourself. Morgan didn't get along with Mom and all of a sudden Mom was murdered. Morgan didn't get along with Emily and now Emily is dead, too!" she exclaimed. "Morgan is the last person to see Emily alive. Don't forget that."

"Come on, Payton. Morgan's not capable of murder. And it doesn't make sense since it was Emily who called her and asked for a swimming lesson. I feel awful that she's dead, but you can't pin this on Morgan."

"About that swimming lesson. Didn't Carter say that Emily supposedly dove off the raft?"

"That's what Morgan told Sheriff Birch. What are you getting at?" she asked with narrowed eyes.

"Doesn't that seem odd to you? In all the years we've known Emily and have gone to the lake with her, when have you ever seen her go to the raft, let alone dive off it. She's not a good swimmer. She'd never go out to the raft. She barely goes into the lake at all."

Raine didn't respond. She thought about what Payton had said. It didn't make sense, but still, she wouldn't believe that Morgan had any part in Emily's death. She'd never gotten into the drama between Payton and Morgan, just as she hadn't with her mother and Morgan. It was obvious that Emily didn't like Morgan, but Raine had to honestly say that she'd never witnessed any cruelty on Morgan's part toward any of them. In fact, Morgan had been nothing but kind toward her and as far as Raine could see, tried hard to be accepted into the family. If anything, she felt sorry for Morgan.

****

Paul carried a cup of tea to Sarah, who lay sprawled out on the living room sofa. "Drink this, sweetie. It'll make you feel better," he soothed.

"I'll try." Slowly she brought the steaming liquid to her trembling lips.

"I've sent Lisa and Terence to Jim and Mary's for the day." Jim and Mary Torrens were the first couple they met when they moved to Vermont. They'd welcomed them to the neighborhood and Paul and Sarah were elated when they discovered their children were near the same ages as Jim and Mary's three. The children all became fast friends. "Jim said he'd bring them back around seven." He felt her forehead. "I want you to rest. Don't worry about anything." He smoothed her hair.

"I'm so upset, Paul. This is too much," she whined. "How much more can one family take?"

"There's nothing we can do to change what's happened," he said softly.

"Morgan was the only one there, Paul." She propped herself up on an elbow. "We barely know her even though she's been with Carter for a few years now. What do we know about her past?"

His eyebrows drew together. "None of us have gone out of our way to try to get to know her, now have we? She's always been decent to me and from what I can see to you, too.

Why does she have to tell us anything about her past? Unless she's hiding some deep dark secret, what does it matter? I, for one, happen to think she's a very nice person," he concluded.

Sarah was thoughtful for a minute. "I suppose you're right." She squeezed her husband's hand. "I'll make an effort to get to know her better." She sipped her tea. "I think I'll try to get some sleep now."

"Good." Paul kissed her forehead.

****

Morgan sat in a lounge chair, thumbing mindlessly through a women's magazine. The words on the pages were all a blur to her and she couldn't concentrate on any of the articles. She was anxious. She knew that Carter believed her about Emily's unfortunate accident, but she sensed Sheriff Birch and that Boston official didn't. She had to be on her guard at all times. She couldn't afford to make one false move.

She looked in Carter's direction. He pulled a squealing Becca in her new red wagon. Every time he laughed, Becca clapped her hands and laughed along with him. Morgan loved her husband so much it hurt and she didn't care what anyone else thought of her, just so long as Carter was by her side. But Carter would leave her if he ever found out what she had done. Once she thought he would understand, but now she wasn't so sure. There were too many people talking about her behind her back and planting seeds of doubt in his mind. He might end up believing the lies they were telling about her. If he did then he'd never be able to look at her without feeling hatred toward her. What would happen to Becca if she were found out? She couldn't bear to have her husband and child taken from her. That would be worse than death. No, she had to keep her cool until everything died down. But that was easier said than done. One thing was certain, though, no one would ever take Carter from her. She wouldn't allow it.

The phone rang and she jumped. She hurried inside the patio door and reached for the phone where it sat on a small table. She grabbed it on the sixth ring. "Hello," she answered breathlessly.

"Is Carter home?"

"Yes, just a minute. Is this Payton?" she asked.

"Yes, I would like to speak to my brother," she replied coldly.

"Okay, I'll get him."

Morgan set the phone down and called to him from the patio door. "Carter, you're wanted on the phone."

Carter picked Becca up out of the wagon. "Who is it?" he asked as he walked to where Morgan waited.

"Payton."

Morgan took Becca's hand. "Come on, honey. Let's have a cookie."

Carter picked up the telephone. "Hello, Payton."

"Hi, Carter. The reason I'm calling is to find out some information about Emily's death."

"She drowned accidentally, Payton. That's all that happened."

"How? I need to know how it happened."

He let his breath out in a huff. "She dove off the raft and didn't come up. Morgan couldn't get to her in time to save her," he explained.

"Was anyone else with Morgan and Emily when it happened?" she questioned.

"What the hell is this, Payton? It sounds to me like an inquisition," he responded angrily.

"Hunter is convinced that Morgan had something to do with Emily's death! I just got off the phone with him a little while ago. I'll be staying at his house and doubt I'll have a chance to talk to you alone." She paused. "You know that Morgan's lying!"

"What the hell are you talking about?" he demanded. "You're hysterical. Hunter is justifiably out of his mind with grief, but that doesn't give him the right to make accusations against my wife. And as for you, I've reached the end of my rope!"

"Carter, if you would just think about this for a minute, I know you would see that the pieces all fit!" Payton said in a calmer tone.

"That's quite enough, Payton!" Carter said firmly. Out of the corner of his eye, he saw Morgan carrying Becca into the room. Becca had an oatmeal cookie clutched tightly in her fist. He smiled at her and then gave Morgan a quick wink.

"Morgan is no good for you, Carter," Payton continued. "She's a cold-blooded murderer! Why can't you see that?" Payton's tone had once again become shrill.

"That's enough! I won't have you or anyone else talk about my wife like that ever again!" He slammed the phone down. "Damn her," he mumbled.

Becca's eyes brimmed with tears, and then she began to cry.

Carter saw the fear in her delicate face. "Oh, baby," he said scooping her into his arms. "Daddy didn't mean to scare you. You know how much Daddy loves you and Mommy," he cooed. He patted her lightly on her back until her sobs subsided. He glanced at Morgan.

"Honey, Becca knows you love her." She softly ran her fingertips across his cheek. "What's gotten you so upset?"

He shrugged. "Nothing. Let's just forget it." He hoisted Becca up on his shoulders. "Daddy's going to give you a ride."

Becca giggled delightedly.

"Let's go see how the flower garden is doing." He smiled. "And then Daddy will give you another ride in your wagon."

"Carter, I want to know what Payton said about me," Morgan insisted.

"Honey, it doesn't matter what Payton or anyone else says or thinks. We love each other and have a bond that can never be broken." He protectively put an arm around her shoulder. "Don't worry about it."

"Carter, please tell me," she pleaded.

He sighed heavily, and then took her hand in his. "She's accusing you of Emily's death. Hunter told her it was deliberate and she believes him."

"She never did like me," she answered in a small voice. "I've tried to be friendly to her, but she pushes me away."

Carter saw the sadness come into her eyes. "Hey, come on. Let her think whatever she wants to. We know the truth." He lovingly squeezed her hand. "Let's cancel our plans to stay with her next month." He frowned. "She probably won't want us to now anyway."

"No, Carter." A tear trickled out of the corner of her eye. "I need to talk to her. By then things should be calmer. Maybe I can convince her to like me. I'm not the demon others seem bent on making me out to be," she said in a trembling voice.

"No, you're not," he murmured.

CHAPTER ELEVEN

Jake Birch leaned back in his chair and rested his feet on his desk. "Any questions, men?" he asked. He gave them a few minutes to absorb the information he'd just given them about Morgan Rogers.

"We really don't have much to go on, do we?" James Wylmer asked as he scratched his head.

"No, but we have to investigate any piece of information that comes in. Especially if it concerns Morgan Rogers," Jake answered.

"Tom's report said that Emily Rogers died from drowning. The autopsy confirmed it," Jason Tismont reasoned. "He can't prove how she got the scratch marks."

"I know, but Morgan Roger's theory about how Emily received the scratch marks doesn't make sense to me." He shook his head. "I don't buy it. How well do you two know Morgan?"

"I don't know her at all," James answered, shrugging his thin shoulders. "I've seen her around town, though."

"I've spoken to her, but only briefly in passing," Jason said. "You don't really think she had anything to do with

141

Emily Rogers drowning, do you?"

Jake rubbed his chin. "Hunter Rogers seems to think so."

"But he didn't witness the drowning," James reminded him. "So he doesn't really know what happened."

"I'm going to question her again. Something doesn't fit."

"Is Boston investigating Emily Rogers' death, too?" Tismont asked.

"Only if there's a link between Rachel Rogers' and Emily Rogers' deaths." He pulled himself to his feet.

****

Carter finished his tuna salad sandwich. He wiped his mouth on a napkin and then threw the napkin on his plate.

"Would you like another one?" Morgan asked. "I made plenty."

"No, I couldn't eat another bite. It was delicious." He smiled as he patted his stomach. "Is Becca sleeping?"

"Yes, she'll probably sleep for another twenty minutes or so." She started to pick up the plates. Carter grabbed her wrist.

"I have an idea," he said. He stood up and gathered her into his arms. "I'd love to take my wife upstairs and make wild, passionate love to her."

She smiled seductively. "Sounds like a wonderful idea," she whispered. "It's been a long time since we've made love in the afternoon."

The doorbell rang and Carter frowned. "Who the hell can that be?"

Morgan slightly lifted her shoulders. "Only one way to

find out."

He saw the disappointment in her eyes as she turned and placed the plates into the dishwasher. "I'll get rid of whoever it is," he promised.

She nodded as she grabbed a sponge and began wiping off the table.

Carter walked to the door as the ringing of the bell continued. "I'm coming," he shouted as he pulled the door open. His jaw tightened when he saw the sheriff and the investigator. "What do you want now?"

"Carter, we have some more questions for Morgan," Jake explained.

"Give me a break. Leave her alone. She's already told you everything there is to tell about Emily's drowning," he answered coldly.

"Maybe she remembered something else," Jake said.

"She didn't."

"Would you get her for us, please?" the sheriff insisted.

"If I don't?" Carter asked.

"We can handle this downtown," Jake said firmly.

Carter held the door wide and led the men into the living room. "Morgan, will you please come in here," he called.

"What is it, honey?" Morgan asked as she entered the living room. She stopped, surprised to see Jake Birch and Mark Barlow seated on the sofa. Their eyes focused on her and she nodded slightly at them. "What can I do for you now?" she asked in an annoyed tone of voice.

"There are a few more questions we need to ask you concerning your sister-in-law's death," Jake stated.

143

"Let's get one thing straight, Jake," Carter interrupted. "I won't allow my wife to be intimidated."

"That's not our intention."

"It's okay, Carter. I have nothing to hide," Morgan responded.

Jake carefully eyed Morgan as he ran his hand over his smooth-shaven face. "Did you know that Emily couldn't swim?"

Morgan walked over to the rocking chair and sat down. She folded her hands in her lap. "I was under the impression that she could swim a little but needed a few lessons."

"Okay, but why would you take someone who was a poor swimmer behind the raft, where the water is obviously deeper than it is on the other side?" He shook his head. "Wouldn't it make more sense to start her off where she would be at ease? Closer to the edge of the lake instead?"

Morgan felt his eyes on her. Maybe he'd like to see more thigh. She had beautiful, well-shaped legs and she knew she looked curvaceous in her too-tight shorts. Men always leered at her that way. She never invited their gawking stares but used them to her advantage whenever she had to. It had worked with Carter and still did. That's why he'd wanted to take her to bed this afternoon before they were so rudely interrupted. She twisted her necklace. "Since I didn't realize she couldn't swim at all, I thought it would be better behind the raft. She could move with more freedom and I would be able to help her. If I had known, then I never would have taken her behind the raft." She looked evenly at him as she awaited his reply. She glanced at Mark Barlow. His gaze was fixated on her chest. She knew he could see her braless, firm, well-rounded breasts through the low-cut blouse she wore. She caught his eye, forcing him to quickly look away.

"Previously you said that Emily dived off the raft," Jake said.

"She did," Morgan answered.

"Why would she do that if she knew she couldn't swim?"

"I have no idea what she was thinking," Morgan retorted. "I suppose she didn't want me to know how limited she truly was."

Mark Barlow crossed his legs. "Tell us from start to finish the events that preceded Emily Rogers' drowning on June fifth."

Morgan felt his cold eyes glaring into her own.

"She's already told you everything that happened!" Carter said, infuriated.

"Listen, Carter, if she chooses not to answer our questions, then that's her right. But let me warn you," Jake said, pointing a finger, "I will take her downtown if she refuses to answer them."

"Maybe we should call our lawyer," Carter said.

"That's your prerogative." Jake shifted his weight. "I'm trying to save us both the time and expense, in your case of obtaining a lawyer, by wrapping this case up now once and for all."

Morgan cleared her throat as she looked at her husband. "Carter, it's all right, honey. As I've stated repeatedly, I have nothing to hide." Her voice was soft.

Carter frowned. "Fine," he answered, even though his tone of voice convinced Morgan that he still wasn't comfortable without legal representation. "Could I ask a question?" He peered at the men.

"Of course," Jake said.

"Am I correct in my assumption that the autopsy proved Emily drowned?"

"That's what the autopsy showed."

He threw his hands up. "Then why are you badgering my wife?"

Jake slowly exhaled. "Carter, I'm going to be straight with you. We can't discount Hunter's statement. We have to investigate his accusations."

Carter jumped to his feet. "Oh, I get it!" he shouted. "Hunter was obviously in shock due to his grief, so you automatically believe him!" He shook his head in wonder. "The next thing you're going to tell me is that you think my wife planted a bomb in my mother's house." He laughed sarcastically. "I don't believe this, Jake. You've known me all my life, yet you come into my home and practically accuse my wife of murdering my family." He trembled with anger. "Has it ever occurred to you that we're grieving, too?"

Morgan jumped out of the chair and ran to his side grabbing his arm. "Please calm down, honey. They obviously don't care about our feelings." She directed her eyes to Mark Barlow. "I'll answer any questions you have and then maybe you'll leave us alone to mourn in peace."

Carter sat on the love seat and pulled Morgan down next to him. "I still don't like it."

"None of us do, Carter," Jake said and then turned his attention back to Morgan. "Start from your walk to the lake with Emily. What did you two talk about?"

146

Morgan eyed him coolly. "We talked about our summer plans, discussed our kids, and things like that. The usual things women talk about when they get together."

"So it was a friendly conversation," Jake said.

"Yes, it was. We'd never been close, but when Emily invited us to go to the lake and asked for the swimming lessons, I knew it was the perfect chance for Emily and me to really get to know one another."

"Did you talk for several minutes?"

She shrugged her shoulders. "I suppose. We talked on our walk down the path and when we reached the lake, we spread our beach towels and talked for a while longer."

"Did Emily ever mention her fear of water?"

"I already answered that. No, she did not."

"What happened next?"

"After a few minutes, I told Emily that I was going to swim over to the raft and she could go into the water when she was ready. She said she would swim to the raft with me, so we swam over together. When we reached the raft, we climbed on and just sat for a short time, looking at the lake. It was a peaceful day."

"There's still something I don't understand," Jake said thoughtfully. "Correct me if I'm wrong, but if Emily could barely swim, then how could she swim with you to the raft?"

Morgan looked directly into Sheriff Birch's eyes, at the same time feeling Mark and Carter's eyes on her. She smiled weakly. "It wasn't exactly swimming, I suppose, now that I think about it. But she did swim a little and then waded."

Jake continued staring at her. "Okay, so what happened after you sat for a while on the raft?"

147

She was thoughtful for a minute. "I told her I would dive in and she could watch me, then I would help her into the water so I could evaluate exactly how much experience she actually had."

Jake frowned. "You had no idea she was going to dive in after you?"

She shook her head emphatically. "No, I would have stopped her if I had known."

"What happened next?"

She shuddered, closed her eyes for a few seconds, and then popped them back open. "I dove in and had just resurfaced when I saw her go into the water," she answered in a shaky voice. "I waited for a few seconds for her to resurface and when she didn't, I dove underwater to search for her." She bit her trembling bottom lip. "It seemed like it took forever to locate her and I struggled to bring her to the surface. When I did, she wasn't responsive so I screamed for Carter and Hunter." She sniffed. "I didn't know if they heard me or not, but I knew I had to get her help. It wasn't easy, but I managed to swim with her to the bank." She covered her face with her hands. "I did try to save her!" she moaned. "I really did." She dabbed at her eyes. "That's what happened. I swear to you that I'm telling you the truth." She looked at the men. From the expression on their faces, she knew they didn't believe a word she'd said. It didn't matter, she reasoned with herself. They had nothing on her. But she had to keep up the façade to be on the safe side. The truth was that she loathed Emily even more in death since the bitch was bringing these problems on her. As for Hunter, someday he'd be sorry for what he'd done to her.

148

"One more question," Mark said. "Why did Hunter try to choke you?"

"He needed to lash out at someone and since I was the last person to see Emily alive, he chose me to take his pain out on." She cleared her throat. "I may be mistaken, but I believe I answered that question before, too." She watched as the men got to their feet.

Jake didn't respond, but instead said, "I guess this wraps it up."

"Thank you for your time," Mark said.

"You're welcome," Morgan said sweetly and then walked out of the room.

"I trust that this will be the last time my wife will be questioned about Emily's drowning," Carter stated as he walked them to the door. "I'd like to think you're putting as much effort into finding my mother's murderer."

"It's top priority, Carter. It always has been," Jake said.

****

"Are you sure you'll be okay?" Carter asked.

"I'll be fine." She looked at him with tear-filled eyes. "Hunter doesn't want me there and I don't want to do anything to add to his pain." She sighed. "It's too bad that Collin and Jude and Paul and Sarah weren't able to come. They had intended to."

"I know. They felt horrible after telling Hunter they'd be there. If they weren't so far away they would have been able to make it to the service, but since a sister-in-law doesn't count as immediate family, with the travel time, they couldn't do it."

"I hope Hunter understands."

"He does. It's good that he has Raine and Payton with him."

"How were they able to get away?"

"They took their vacation time. I was happy they were able to get the day off and together. He needs all the support he can get."

"I'd ask you to give him my love, but he'd just throw it back at you."

"I've got to go." He gave her a quick hug.

****

Carter grabbed a beer from Hunter's refrigerator. Most of those who'd stopped by Hunter's house after the services had left. Raine and Payton were busy putting food away and tidying up the kitchen.

"Can I talk to you a minute, Payton?" Carter asked pulling out a chair at the kitchen table and seating himself.

"Sure." She joined him at the table.

He took a swallow of beer. "I was thinking maybe Morgan and I should cancel our plans to visit you."

"Why?"

He lifted his eyebrows in surprise. "You've made it perfectly clear how you feel about her."

Raine joined them at the table. "If I had the room you could stay with me."

"Thank you, Raine. I suppose we could stay at a hotel. Morgan is excited about the art show. I hate to disappoint her."

"No," Payton broke in. "I want you to stay with me. I promise to be on my best behavior. You said that Emily and Morgan were trying to make peace so it's about time that I

150

did, too." Tears brimmed in her eyes. "I don't want to lose any more family by death or other means."

"Thank you, Payton," Carter replied.

Hunter walked into the kitchen, over to the fridge, grabbed a beer, and joined them at the table.

"How you holding up?" Carter asked him.

He exhaled loudly. "Every time I come in here I expect to see Emily at the stove." He slowly shook his head. "I never realized how much time she spent in here."

"Cooking was her passion," Payton said.

"Yeah," he said. He slightly rolled the beer bottle between his hands.

"It was a nice service, Hunter," Raine said.

"Her parents did most of the planning."

"Are the kids spending the night with Emily's parents?" Carter asked.

He nodded. "I want them to spend as much time with them as they can." His forehead furrowed.

"So you've made the decision?" Carter asked.

"What decision?" Raine and Payton asked simultaneously.

"Before Emily…" He stopped to clear his throat. "We had discussed an offer I had received and had decided I'd turn it down. She didn't want to leave Weldon and her parents. Which was fine by me. But now I think I need to take the offer. I can't stay in this house now so I accepted the offer. I don't have to leave for a while. It'll give me time to put the house on the market. I haven't discussed it with Emily's parents yet and I'm not looking forward to it."

Payton began sobbing. "What's happening to our

family?"

"Where's the job, Hunter?" Raine asked.

"In California."

"Wipe your eyes, Payton. Our next vacation will be in California," Raine said lightening the mood.

A faint smile broke across Hunter's face. "I'll look forward to it."

"Okay, I want details," Raine said.

"Well, it pays almost twice what I'm making now. But of course, I have to factor in that the cost of living will be higher in California than it is here."

Carter sat back sipping at his beer while he watched his sisters and brother. He'd be the only one left from the family residing in Weldon. How sad, he thought. His parents had loved it here and had assumed their children would spend their lives here. But times were different and they had to each live their own lives.

He'd miss Hunter and regretted the lost years they'd never get back again. He wished he could turn back time.

CHAPTER TWELVE

Jake opened the window in his office, but there was no breeze or relief from the stifling heat. The air hung thick and heavy. The ceiling fan didn't help. It was only ten o'clock in the morning and the temperature had already risen to eighty-two degrees. Maintenance was working on the air conditioning and Jake hoped it would be repaired soon.

He looked at the calendar. It was hard to believe that over three weeks had passed since Emily Rogers' death. Things seemed to be settling back into a normal mode in Weldon. The old familiar pattern of life emerged once again and the locals weren't as edgy as they had been right after Rachel Rogers was murdered. He glanced at the two well-worn folders, which still had the position of top priority, lying on his desk. *Will we ever learn the truth about your deaths?* he wondered. He sat down at his desk.

Jake thought about the long hours he and Mark Barlow had put into this investigation. They were definitely on the same page where Morgan Rogers was concerned. He'd grown fond of the investigator and they'd shared many dinners together talking about the two cases. Barlow wasn't pleased when he'd been given orders to return to Boston. Two weeks ago he left, but not before giving Jake strict orders to contact him the minute anything out of the ordinary occurred in the Rogers' family. He warned Jake to keep especially close tabs on Morgan Rogers. Jake heeded his advice, but Morgan was a slick one. She appeared to anyone who saw her as the perfect wife and mother. He would get her, though. Eventually she'd make the wrong move and he'd be there. Then these cases would be put to rest.

****

Becca bounced happily up and down on Morgan's lap as Carter grabbed his sunglasses.

"I should've gotten the damned air-conditioning fixed," he grumbled. "We'll roast."

Morgan affectionately squeezed his arm. "It's not that bad, honey. Let me drive and you can relax."

"I don't think so." He grinned. "We'd better get the baby in her car seat."

"Why don't you want me to drive?" she asked.

He grinned. "Honey, I want to get to my destination in one piece."

She playfully slapped his arm. "You take care of the rest of the luggage and I'll get her strapped in."

"Okay." He grabbed two suitcases and maneuvered them into the back. Morgan sat Becca in the car seat and buckled her in, handing her a few toys and a cookie.

"All set?" Carter asked, coming around to the passenger side.

Morgan nodded. "All set, but I still think you should let me drive."

154

"No, I value my life too much," he teased.

"You wait, Carter Rogers, you'll get yours," she laughed.

He raised his eyebrows as he slid into the driver's seat. "Is that a promise?"

She winked. She was filled with anticipation and excitement. She planned to thoroughly enjoy their vacation in Portland. Sheriff Birch had stayed true to his word and left her alone. She'd heard that the investigator had completed his work and had left Weldon. Life was getting back to normal. She was safe. If he had anything on her, he would have made his move by now. Everything was falling into place as planned. Whenever that damning paranoia crept into her mind, she chased it out. She hated the feeling it gave her. She flicked on the radio and tuned in an easy listening station, singing along with the song.

Carter glanced over at her. "I hope you're not planning to make a career move," he quipped. She scowled. "Oh darn, now you've ruined my surprise! I was going to make a recording for you." She laughed.

"Heaven forbid!"

****

Jude lay on a lounger in her backyard. Collin knelt beside her, offering one of the cans of beer he held in his hands. Jude shaded her eyes as she watched Kurt, Sandra, and Susie play a game of kickball.

Collin stretched out in a lounger next to her. "You look a little down today. Are you feeling all right?"

"I'm fine," she answered with a smile. "I was just thinking about Carter and Morgan's visit a couple of weeks

155

ago."

Collin sensed the uneasiness in her voice. "I thought the visit was very enjoyable."

"I did, too, but there was something different about Morgan."

He shrugged his shoulders. "She seemed more relaxed than I've ever seen her."

She shook her head. "No, it was her personality. She seemed...different somehow...invincible."

"I guess I didn't pick up on it," Collin said.

"Weren't you surprised they wanted to visit? I knew they were planning to go to Portland to spend a weekend with the girls and then go to Vermont to see Paul and Sarah. Why all the visits lately? We rarely have seen them since we've moved."

"Maybe the deaths have changed her and she wants to get closer to everyone."

"I suppose that could be it." She eyed her husband. "I know she's extremely possessive of Carter and the baby. Even talking to her, she seemed different. Not like someone who is trying to get closer to the family."

He frowned. "The deaths have taken a toll on all of us. I suppose we all handle death in our own way."

"It's different with her. It's like she's building a wall around herself and dragging Carter and Becca behind it with her and doesn't want to let anyone in. I've always been close to her, but I couldn't even penetrate it."

Collin chuckled. "You know that Carter and Morgan idolize each other. They've always lived in their own private little world."

"I know that, Collin," she said hastily. "But something didn't feel right."

He sighed. "I suppose we can't blame her for being protective after Jake and…what was that investigator's name?"

"Barlow."

"Yeah, Barlow…those two dragged her through the mill. That's got to wear anyone down."

"If she's innocent then why should it bother her?" Jude frowned. "And why do they keep questioning her? Do they know something they're not telling us?"

"I don't know." He shook his head. "Maybe she's not as innocent as we think she is."

"Collin!" she snapped. "How can you think such a thing?"

His eyes narrowed. "You said it, not me."

"I guess I'm letting my imagination get the better of me. Of course she had nothing to do with either death." She patted his hand. "Still, she's just not the same Morgan I know and love. She used to be so lively and fun to be with, but it's like life has soured for her and she doesn't care about anyone except Carter and Becca."

"She hasn't shown much emotion concerning the deaths," he agreed. "But the family hasn't treated her very well either."

"I'm ashamed for thinking badly of her, Collin, but she's critical of everything lately. I suppose, though, that I'd be angry too, if I were being hounded by Jake and that Barlow." She pursed her lips. "It had to be horrible for her to see Emily drown."

Before Collin could comment, Sandra ran to them. She stood above them, laughingly dripping water on their heads.

"Honey, dry yourself," Collin laughed as he threw her a beach towel. "I thought you kids were playing ball."

"We were, but it got too hot so Kurt squirted us with the hose." She ran the towel over her legs. "When we gonna eat?"

Collin pulled himself to his feet. "I'll put the hamburgers on the grill in a few minutes." He reached down and grabbed Jude's hands. "Time to feed our hungry bunch."

****

Payton rushed around her apartment dusting and vacuuming. When her chores were finished, she wearily threw herself into an easy chair. She looked at the clock. Eleven forty-five. Carter and Morgan would be here shortly. She closed her eyes, wishing it were cooler in her hot, sticky apartment.

She heard a noise outside her door. She ran to it, flung it wide open, and threw herself into her brother's arms. "You're looking well," she said with a bright smile. "Come on in."

"Hello, Payton."

"Hi, Morgan. I'm sorry, I didn't mean to ignore you." She flashed a weak smile. "Hi, Becca," she said chucking the child under the chin. Carter set the suitcases down.

"Let me take them into the bedroom for you, Carter. Sit down and make yourselves comfortable," Payton said as she grabbed the suitcases.

Carter stretched out on the sofa. "This feels good," he sighed contentedly.

Becca played with some toys on the floor and Morgan

158

seated herself in an old rocking chair.

"It sure is a scorcher today," Payton announced as she returned to the room.

"You can say that again," Carter agreed.

"Was there a lot of traffic, Carter?" she asked.

"Actually, there wasn't. I assumed the roads would be clogged with travelers hitting the beaches." He yawned.

"How about a cold drink?" she offered.

"That would hit the spot," he answered.

"What about you, Morgan?" Payton smiled.

"I'd love one," she replied with an easy smile.

"I'll be right back," Payton said, excusing herself.

Carter relaxed. Payton seemed to have put her incriminating remarks about Morgan behind her. Maybe she was indeed ready to make a fresh start. He pulled himself to a sitting position. "Come sit next to me," he beckoned to Morgan.

Morgan got out of the rocking chair and moved to the sofa sitting down next to him. She grabbed his hand.

"I love you," he whispered.

She smiled. "I love you, too."

His gaze traveled over her. "Did I tell you how sexy you look today?"

She shook her head. "I doubt that. I'm all sweaty and sticky."

His hand traveled over her arm, then rested on her breast. "This feels nice," he said in her ear.

"Carter," she blushed, slapping his hand away. "Remember where we are," she warned.

"Caught you!" Payton said with a laugh as she carried

a tray of drinks, cheese, and crackers and set them on the small coffee table.

Carter grinned and then winked. "We're married, so we can get away with it."

Becca spied the cheese and crackers and ran to them, arms outstretched.

Carter put a piece of cheese on a cracker and handed it to her.

"What time do you want to go to the art show?" Payton asked as she poured their drinks.

Carter leaned forward. "Morgan wants to see a lot of art, which doesn't mean a damn thing to me, so I'm letting her take the car. You and I can take Becca to Two Lights or anywhere you'd like to go. Unless you want to go to the show."

"I've never been much into art." She looked at Morgan. "You don't mind, do you?"

"Of course not," Morgan answered softly. "I think it'll be nice for you and Carter to have some time together."

Payton returned her smile. "Good. That's settled then. Two Lights is fine with me," Payton answered. "What time do you want to go?"

"About two?" he asked.

"Okay."

Carter put an arm around Morgan's shoulders and gave her a tender squeeze.

****

Morgan parked the car in the public parking garage. She looked at the ticket, stamped 2:22 PM. She stuffed the ticket into her jeans pocket, and then headed down Congress

160

Street. Occasionally she stopped to look at an exhibit. Every few minutes she glanced at her wristwatch. Anticipation mounted in her, and her stomach was filled with butterflies. She had to be certain Carter and Payton were well on their way.

A painting caught her eye and she asked its bearded creator the price of his masterpiece. When he said $450, she shook her head and walked on.

She stopped in a bar and ordered a seven and seven. She sipped at her drink, every few minutes her eyes darting to the large Budweiser clock hanging behind the bar. The minutes crawled by. Her impatience rose.

She finished her drink and ordered another. She noticed an attractive man making his way toward her, but she pretended she didn't see him.

"Can I buy you a drink?" he offered.

"No, thank you." She stared into her glass.

"What's your name? I haven't seen you in here before."

"I'm just here for the weekend—with my husband." She emphasized *my husband,* hoping that would scare him off.

He cleared his throat. "So where is he?" he asked, glancing around the small room.

"He'll be here shortly."

"Well, until he gets here, why don't you and I get to know one another?"

She raised her eyes level to his and flashed him an angry look. "I'm not interested. Please leave me alone!" Her voice was firm.

"Okay, okay," he answered, putting his hands up in protest. "No need to make a scene." He retrieved his former seat at the end of the bar.

Probably waiting for his next victim, Morgan thought as she drained her second drink. She looked again at the Budweiser clock. It was four o'clock now. She slid off the bar stool and walked outside into the glaring sunlight. She walked for what seemed like miles, but was only a few blocks. She finally found a taxi and quickly got in. She gave the driver an address about a block from Payton's apartment building.

Morgan waited until the driver sped away, and then walked briskly until she reached Payton's building. She cautiously looked around before entering the building. She walked up the stairs and stood in front of the door, fumbling inside her purse for the key Payton had given her before she left. She breathed a sigh of relief when she found it, then hurriedly inserted it into the lock. She opened the door and slipped inside.

Forty-five minutes later, she left the apartment.

****

Payton stood in the dim hallway, keys jingling on their key ring. "It was nice this afternoon, Carter," she said.

He smiled at his sister. "Yes, it was." He shifted a sleeping Becca to his other arm. "She really tired herself out today. But she'll sleep good tonight," he said, nodding at his daughter. "I could use a nap myself." He yawned.

Payton laughed. "Me, too." She softly ran her fingertips over Becca's bare arm. "She didn't get burned too badly, did she?"

"Not as bad as I did. Morgan will kill me for forgetting to put the sunblock on."

"We'd better get Becca into bed," Payton said as she

162

inserted her key into the lock. She slowly opened the door and flicked on the light.

Her keys fell to the floor as a piercing scream escaped from her throat. "Oh my God!"

Her scream awoke Becca, who began to cry.

"Payton, what's wrong?" Carter asked as he pushed himself into the room.

Payton stood, pointing at the wall.

Carter made his way into the apartment. The wall had been stripped of its decorations and in large bright red painted letters, a message had been scrawled. It read: *Watch Your Step Bitch!!!* On the floor immediately below the wall was a large dead rat. The color drained from his face. "This is a threat," he said. He glanced around the rest of the room. The desk drawers were open and the contents strewn around the room. He handed Becca to Payton. "Hold her while I check out the rest of the apartment."

"Okay," she replied.

He checked out the rest of the apartment and came back into the living room. "The rest of the apartment is fine," he said.

She trembled. "Who could have done this?" she asked in a wobbly voice. "And why?"

"I don't know." He studied the childishly scrawled message again. "Payton, take Becca into the bedroom and I'll call the police."

"Can you get rid of the rat, Carter?"

"We'd better wait until the police see it."

She nodded and carried Becca to the bedroom.

Carter was hanging up the phone when Payton walked

back into the room. "The police are on their way." He rubbed his eyes. "Have you recently had an argument with anyone, Payton? At work or someone in the building?"

"No. I can't think of anyone who would do this. I haven't had any run-ins with anyone."

Moments later Carter ushered two policemen into the apartment.

"Do you have any idea who could have done this?" the taller officer asked Payton. "An ex-boyfriend?"

"No," she whispered in a muffled voice.

"Have you had any confrontations lately with anyone?"

She shook her head. "No."

"How long were you gone from the apartment today?"

"My brother and I left about two-thirty this afternoon and returned about twenty minutes ago."

"What is your name?" the shorter officer asked Carter.

"I'm her brother, Carter," he answered. "I'm here with my wife and daughter visiting for the weekend."

The officer examined the door. "It wasn't a forced entry," he said. "Does anyone else have a key to your apartment?"

"No." She blew her nose loudly and then added, "I did give a spare key to my brother's wife. She's at the art show."

He jotted the information down. "When do you expect her to return?"

As if on cue, Morgan entered the room, her eyes widening at the sight of the policemen. "What's happened?"

"Who are you?" the shorter officer asked.

"Morgan Rogers," she answered.

"Do you have a key to this apartment?"

"Yes." She looked at Carter. "Why?"

"Did you return here at all this afternoon?"

"No, I was at the art show all day."

"Can you prove it?" He stared into her eyes.

"Just a minute, officer," Carter cut in. "Why are you questioning my wife about this?"

"I'm just trying to establish whether she came back this afternoon. If she did, she may have seen someone lurking around the building," he explained.

"I didn't come back," Morgan answered. "And, yes, I can prove it," she said, pulling the parking ticket from her pocket and handing it to the officer.

He looked at the ticket. "You were parked from 2:22 until 7:13 p.m." He looked into her eyes. "Okay." He returned the ticket to her. He then turned to Carter. "Are you any relation to the Rogers from Weldon, Massachusetts?"

Carter nodded. "Yes, my mother's home was bombed."

"I'm sorry," the officer replied.

Morgan clutched her package tightly. She shuddered when she saw the rat and then read the message on the wall. "How horrible!"

The taller officer turned his attention back to Payton. "Is anything missing?"

"I don't know. I don't think so. I only had papers in the desk along with notebooks and pens."

"Nothing was disturbed in the other rooms. I checked them," Carter added.

"Let us know if you notice anything missing," the officer said. "You can clean that up," he said, pointing to the dead rat.

"I'll take care of it," Carter said.

"We'll be in touch with you," he said to Payton.

"Thank you," she said in a barely audible voice. Her eyes drifted back to the wall. "I don't know anyone who would do this."

"Call us if anything else happens," the taller officer said.

Carter closed the door behind the officers, and then walked over to the sofa where Payton sobbed uncontrollably. He sat next to her, cradling her in his arms until she calmed down. "I'll get this cleaned up." He went into the kitchen and grabbed a box of plastic bags and a can of rug cleaner.

As he placed the rat in a plastic bag, he caught Morgan's eye. "What kind of sick asshole would do something like this?"

"It's unthinkable, honey," Morgan whispered. "Is Becca sleeping?"

"Yes, she fell asleep on the way home. She had a good time today. I wish you could've seen her."

"Did you go to Two Lights?"

"Yeah."

"Did Becca eat dinner?"

"We stopped at a restaurant," he replied, bending to observe the stained carpet.

"What did she eat?"

He smiled. "What else? Her favorite...spaghetti. You should've seen her eating it." He laughed. "I should've taken a picture. She managed to pack quite a bit of it away, though."

Morgan chuckled. "Well, that's my girl." She grabbed the can of rug cleaner and sprayed the spot that had just been vacated by the dead rat.

Payton began picking up the papers, pens, and notebooks and placed them back into the desk. "I'll have to get some paint for the wall."

"Do you have any left from when you painted last winter?"

"I'll check the storage area in the basement." She walked to the door and then turned when she saw Morgan scrubbing the carpet. "Thank you for cleaning that, Morgan."

"No problem. I'm just grateful that we were here to help you."

"I'll be back in a few minutes," she said.

Carter tied up the plastic bag and looked at the wall. "A coat of paint should take care of it."

"It looks like no stain from the rat," Morgan said standing up. "Would you like to see what I bought?" she asked eagerly.

"I sure would," he replied.

"Let me wash my hands first." After she finished, she came back and picked up her package. She slowly unwrapped it and then held it up for him to see.

Carter carefully scrutinized the painting of Portland Harbor at sunset. "It's beautifully done. The artist certainly captured all the intricate details." He leaned toward her. "I'm almost afraid to ask, but how much was it?"

Her eyes glowed. "Would you believe just seventy-five dollars? He wanted one twenty-five, but I talked him down."

"Good for you! This will look great in the living room."

Morgan smiled, pleased with herself. "Do you think Payton would mind if I take a quick shower?"

"No, go ahead."

****

The apartment was silent. Morgan leaned over Carter. His even breathing told her he was in a deep slumber. She quietly slipped out of bed and tiptoed into the darkened living room. She pushed a button on her wristwatch. The illuminated numbers read 3:31. She would have to be quick or Carter may awaken and wonder where she was.

Payton was sound asleep on her pull-out sofa. She'd be out for hours. They'd managed to get the wall repainted and it looked as good as new. Morgan had excused herself when the painting was completed and gone off to bed. Carter and Payton had sat up talking while Payton polished off an entire bottle of wine.

Morgan quietly opened the door, making sure to fix the lock so she could get back inside. Earlier she had returned Payton's spare key to her. She quietly hurried downstairs. Payton's car was parked next to her and Carter's. She gazed up and down the deserted street. When she was satisfied that she was totally alone, she opened the trunk of her car and removed Carter's hacksaw blade from his toolbox.

She went about her business, expertly slicing the brake line to Payton's car. "After today, Payton, you'll never be able to hurt me again," she whispered. She took a deep breath, enjoying the early morning coolness, and then smiled as she gazed up at the star-filled sky.

When she finished, she hurried back into the apartment and slipped into bed beside Carter. He hadn't stirred from the position in which she left him.

****

Carter and Payton sat at Payton's small kitchen table, drinking coffee and munching on glazed doughnuts when Morgan came into the room. She yawned as she wrapped her robe tighter around herself. "Where's Becca?" she asked.

"Under here." Carter motioned under the table.

Morgan dropped to her knees and peered under it. Becca sat between Carter and Payton's feet, happily chewing on a doughnut. She laughed as she patted her daughter's head.

"Want some coffee, hon?" Carter asked.

"Sure, I'll get it," she said and stood.

"Did you sleep okay, Morgan?" Payton asked.

"Like a baby." She flashed Payton a bright smile.

Payton stared into her coffee cup. For a minute, Morgan thought she was going to burst into tears again.

Carter looked at Morgan, and then Payton. Morgan wondered what he was thinking. He had a contented look on his face. *He probably thinks we're one big happy family now*, she thought.

Payton stood up, then pushed her chair in, making certain Becca was out of the way. "Well, I have to be on my way," she announced in a heavy voice. "I have to go in earlier than usual today, but I should be home around two. I'm sure Raine will stop by for a visit this morning. She lucked out and got the day off since she'd requested it ages ago."

"It's too bad you have to work on a Sunday," Carter said.

"I know, but that's when all the shoppers have time. Weekends are the busiest...and holidays." She grimaced.

"Do you want me to fill Raine in on what happened last night?"

169

"Sure. I'm grateful that you two were here. I don't know what I would have done since Raine was out of town at a concert."

"We'll go somewhere special for dinner tonight," Carter promised. "I'll invite Raine, too."

"That would be nice," she replied.

Morgan poured herself a cup of coffee. It wouldn't be long now. She felt the anticipation rising within her. She looked up and flashed Payton another bright smile. "Have a nice day."

"See you two later," Payton said as she grabbed her car keys from the hook.

****

Payton stepped into her car, started it, and eased into traffic. When she stepped on the brake, she noticed a pull. She flicked on the radio and hummed along to the tune as she sped down the street. She stopped for a stop sign and felt the brake pull again. She continued for a couple more miles, noticing how every stop became more difficult. She really needed to take the car in now. Once she got to a garage, she'd call Carter and ask him to pick her up and drop her at work. She'd also let her boss know what had happened and she'd be a little late. She didn't relish having to take a bus to work, but she'd have no choice.

She wished there weren't so many hills to navigate—especially the one she had to climb to reach the garage that she knew would be open, at the bottom. She could go around and come up via the expressway, but that might be too dangerous with her braking situation. She stepped on the accelerator, trying to gain the momentum to make her climb. She reached the top of the hill, and then began her descent. She pumped the brake as she sped down the incline. She wasn't slowing so she slammed her foot to the floor. The brake was gone. Her heart leaped into her throat. Even if she could control the car, a sharp curve lay at the bottom. She grabbed the emergency brake, pulling on it with all her strength as she kept a grip on the steering wheel with her other hand. The emergency brake was inactive. She continued to pump the brake as panic overtook her. "No!" she cried as she frantically willed the emergency brake to halt her vehicle.

She tried desperately to keep the car under her control, but she was fighting a losing battle. She knew it. Tears streamed down her face. This was it. She tried to swerve as the guardrail came into view, but it was too late to make the turn. She flung her hands over her face just before hitting the guardrail and careening down the embankment.

****

Raine scratched her head thoughtfully. "I can't think of anyone who would be sick enough to put a dead rat in someone's house. The person is obviously crazy."

"It was horrible," Morgan answered.

"But why Payton?" Raine questioned.

Carter rubbed his eyes. "It doesn't make sense, but then, not much has in these past couple of months."

"It's like a curse has been put on the family," Raine said quietly.

Morgan poured more coffee. "Maybe I should cancel my plans for the art show this afternoon." She looked at Carter, hoping he would pick up on the disappointment in her voice.

"No," Carter said firmly. "You've been looking forward to this weekend and you're going to enjoy yourself."

Morgan sighed. "It's so frustrating wondering why and who could be doing this." She shuddered.

Carter let his breath out in a rush. "Well, I'm not going to let him ruin our weekend. So, Raine, we're planning to go out to dinner tonight. We want you to come, too."

She nodded. "Thanks, I'd love to." She swallowed hard. "Carter, do you think what happened here last night has any connection to Mom's murder? I mean, was that message a warning?"

"I don't know. It could just be a coincidence."

"But that's not what you really think, is it, Carter?"

"No. What I can't figure out, though, is what the motive is. Is there even a motive or was our family just randomly targeted? Then I wonder if it's someone we know…someone we see every day. I've gone over it a hundred times in my mind looking for a connection, anything that may be a clue." He frowned. "It's getting to the point where I'm nervous about going to work and leaving Morgan and Becca alone," he confided.

"Emily drowned, Carter. She wasn't murdered," Morgan gently reminded him.

Carter scrunched up his face. "I know, honey, but it's just the fact that we've had two deaths in the family within weeks. You've got to admit it's pretty unnerving," he insisted.

Raine slowly shook her head back and forth. "Sometimes I forget Mom's dead, and I'll pick up the phone and dial her number."

"I know," Carter said softly. "I've done the same

172

thing." He finished his coffee. "Is Payton still seeing Johnny Todd? She hasn't mentioned him, and I didn't want to bring his name up if things weren't working out for them."

"Yeah, she's still seeing him, but I sometimes wonder where their relationship will lead."

"What do you mean?"

She frowned. "I don't think Johnny wants to make a serious commitment."

The phone rang. "Maybe he'll change his mind," Carter answered as he grabbed the phone. "Hello…yes, Officer. Payton Rogers is my sister. My wife and I are spending the weekend with her." He paused. "Yes, Raine is also my sister."

Raine was on her feet and at Carter's side. She grabbed his arm. "What's wrong, Carter?" she asked, alarm rising in her voice. Carter raised a hand to silence her and briefly covered the phone with his other hand. "It's probably about last night." He listened to the caller for a minute. "Yes, I'll be waiting for you," he said in a shaky voice as he set the phone down. His hand trembled.

"What is it, Carter?" Raine demanded shrilly. "Has something happened?"

He squeezed his eyes shut, and then slowly opened them. "I don't know. I mean, he really didn't say," he answered. "He was very vague."

"What *did* he say, honey?" Morgan asked. "He must have said something or you wouldn't be so upset."

He looked at his wife. "He asked me if I knew Payton. He tried calling Raine but couldn't get an answer. He's coming over." Carter inhaled deeply as he wearily ran his hand through his hair. "I have a bad feeling about this." He

173

looked at his sister. "We'd better brace ourselves for more bad news."

The color drained from Raine's face. "No, Carter! We can't take anymore!" she screamed as he pulled her close to his chest.

CHAPTER THIRTEEN

Carter led the officer into the living room. He pointed to Raine and Morgan, who were seated on the sofa. "This is my sister Raine and my wife, Morgan."

"My name's Detective Tom Bellman," he said, flashing his identification at them.

"Won't you have a seat?" Morgan politely offered.

"No, thank you. I understand that there was an incident here last night?"

"Yes," Carter answered and filled him in.

Detective Bellman's jaw tightened. "I'm afraid I have some bad news for you. Your sister was involved in a car accident this morning."

"No!" Raine screamed.

"How…how is she?" Carter asked.

"I'm sorry. She's dead."

"Dead?" Carter croaked as his face turned deathly white. Raine began to scream and moan hysterically. A tear slid out of the corner of Carter's eye and splashed onto his cheek. He quickly brushed it away. "What happened?" he whispered hoarsely.

"From what we can determine, it looks like her brakes failed. She was near Henderson's Garage, so we assume she was taking her car in for repairs."

"No, she was going to work. She works at the Maine Mall," Carter said. "She never mentioned having car trouble."

"We're just assuming that she was on her way to the garage. Henderson's is located at the bottom of a steep hill. She, in all probability, lost control of the car. There's a sharp curve before the bottom of the hill. She didn't make the turn, but hit the guardrail and proceeded over the embankment."

"It doesn't make sense. Her car was fine yesterday. I even drove her car and the brakes were fine."

"Two gas attendants from Henderson's were eyewitnesses and their report states that the car had to be traveling at least ninety miles per hour before it took the curve." He paused. "We're having the car checked out to see if the brake line was tampered with."

"Do you think there's a connection with what happened last night?"

He frowned. "I honestly don't know. If the brakes were indeed tampered with, then we'll take it from there."

"Are you aware that my mother, Rachel Rogers, was murdered in Weldon, Massachusetts a few weeks ago?"

"Yes, I know about your mother's murder. I'm sorry. We'll look into the possibility that this could be the same person if indeed your sister was murdered. That would shed new light on this case and your mother's."

"How's that?" Carter asked.

"That person may have followed you here." He eyed Carter. "I'm going to call Sheriff Birch and fill him in on the accident."

Carter nodded.

"Again, I'm very sorry for your loss. Is there anything I can do for you and your family?" he offered glancing at Raine and Morgan.

Carter shook his head. "No, thank you."

****

Carter didn't know how he survived the next few days. He contacted the family and made all of the necessary arrangements. They'd all be in Weldon on Wednesday for the funeral. The Craig Funeral Home would handle the preparations for this third funeral, and Payton would be laid to rest in the plot next to her mother and father.

Carter persuaded Raine to stay in Weldon with him and Morgan for as long as she needed to. She gratefully accepted his offer.

Detective Bellman had come back twice to Payton's apartment to talk to Carter and share what little information they had gathered. The report showed signs of tampering on Payton's brake line. Carter had already feared that this was what the report would show. There was no other explanation. Someone wanted his family dead and wouldn't rest until he succeeded in killing them off one by one. But who?

****

Jake Birch phoned Mark Barlow the minute he got off the phone with Detective Bellman to give him the news of Payton Rogers' death.

"Her brake line was sliced," Jake explained.

"Are there any suspects?" Mark asked.

"No, they're going to keep me posted."

"It looks like whoever killed Rachel Rogers killed her daughter, too. Did Payton live alone or was anyone living with her? A boyfriend? Girlfriend?"

"As far as I know she lived alone. Carter and Morgan Rogers were spending the weekend with her."

"Morgan Rogers. It seems like she's always around when tragedy strikes," Mark said dryly.

"But we still have no proof that she's involved," Jake reasoned.

"No, we don't, but I'll bet a month's salary that she is."

"You don't have to convince me," Jake replied.

"She's smart, so we've got to be just a little smarter." He paused. "Do you think Carter would give us any background information on her? Something she may have told him?"

Jake sniffed. "I doubt it. You saw the way he came to her defense when we questioned her about Emily Rogers' drowning."

"I ran a background check on her but didn't come up with anything unusual. I'm going to run a more extensive check. I want to talk to her past acquaintances and see if anyone can shed any light on her."

Jake frowned. "Don't you find it strange that neither Carter nor any of his family knows much about her?"

"What I find strange is the fact that Carter has never questioned her. It doesn't make sense," Mark said.

"He's nuts about her," Jake said.

"So you think he doesn't want to rock the boat?"

"I don't know. Maybe he doesn't want the illusion destroyed."

Mark slowly let his breath out. "His perfect wife may

have a flaw that he can't deal with."

Jake sniffed. "Who knows? All I know for sure is that we have to do something before someone else in that family is killed."

"I'll be in Weldon in a couple of days just as soon as I clear it. Hopefully I'll have some information."

Jake hung up the phone and leaned back in his chair. He rubbed the back of his neck. When would this nightmare end? He thought back to when Payton was a young child. There was never a time that she hadn't greeted him cheerfully and respectfully whenever he passed her way. Now she was dead.

****

Carter stood silently in the cemetery, his family surrounding him. His grief consumed him, but he kept it locked tightly inside. He squeezed Morgan's hand, grateful that a neighborhood girl had volunteered to babysit the children even though Morgan said she would if no one could be found. He looked up at the sky. It was a beautiful shade of blue, giving way to a glorious summer's day. He listened to a bird chirping merrily in a nearby tree as he morosely eyed his family, wondering which one of them would be the next victim. Or would it be him? When Payton's white coffin was lowered into the freshly dug grave, his grief overcame him and he sobbed.

****

Jake Birch and Mark Barlow stood at the back of the crowd of mourners, speaking in hushed tones as they kept their eyes focused on the large crowd. They hoped to catch a glimpse of anyone acting suspicious.

179

Mark Barlow kept his eyes focused on Morgan Rogers, who stood calmly next to her husband. "Have you had a chance to talk to Carter Rogers?"

Jake shook his head. "No, I'm going over tomorrow."

"Good, good. The sooner the better. We have to convince him what we may be up against."

"It won't be easy," Jake cautioned.

"It never is," Mark answered. "It never is."

****

Carter struggled through the day, thinking it would never end. He sank wearily into a chair and looked around the living room at his family. Morgan had gone upstairs to settle Becca for the night.

"Hunter, let me fix you a drink," Carter offered. "Anyone else want one?"

"I don't want a drink, Carter." His eyes narrowed. "You know who's killing off our family," he said desperately. "All of you know who's doing it."

"No, Hunter, I don't, but I wish to hell I did," Carter answered noting his brother's hollow cheeks and ashen complexion.

Hunter's eyes grew wild. "It's that damned wife of yours! That's who!"

His brother's remark took him by surprise. "Hunter, I thought you were over that," Carter said roughly. "You're grasping at straws."

"She *was* in the vicinity when it happened, Carter," Sarah pointed out. "You can't deny that."

Carter angrily shook his head. "I was in the vicinity too, so do you also accuse me?" he retorted. "Some family I have!

Who else thinks my wife is responsible for these deaths?" he demanded, standing up and slowly turning to look intently at each of them.

Collin grabbed his arm. "Calm down, Carter."

Carter pulled his arm free. "It's so easy for you to tell me to calm down, Collin. How the hell would you feel if it was Jude being accused of these crimes?" He glared into his brother's eyes. "How can you all sit there and let my wife be accused of murder?"

Raine walked to Carter's side. "I don't believe that Morgan had anything to do with any of the deaths, Carter." Her voice was gentle.

Carter looked into her warm, compassionate eyes. "Thank you, Raine. It's nice to see there's still someone left in the family who has some common sense."

Collin shook his head. "Carter, Jude and I certainly haven't entertained the thought that Morgan could in any way be responsible."

Carter looked at Jude. She flashed him a weak smile, then lowered her eyes.

****

Morgan sat on the edge of her bed. She scanned the list of names on the paper she tightly held in her hand until her eyes settled on Payton's name. "Finally," she whispered triumphantly. She wrote next to Payton's name: "Completed July 11, 1983." A sense of well-being surged through her, making her almost giddy. She laughed out loud and then quickly covered her mouth with her hand so no one would hear her. If she'd been caught laughing that would certainly need an explanation, but she supposed she could always say she was remembering some cute little thing Becca had done. She put the list back into its hiding place, and then shoved the metal box back under the nightstand.

She gazed at her reflection in the mirror. Sometimes she didn't recognize the face staring back at her and she had to remember it really was her. She fluffed her hair and turned away from the mirror. Her reflection sometimes made her nervous, just like strangers did when they looked too intently at her. She grinned. She didn't mind people looking at her to admire her beauty, just so they didn't look too long or too hard. She was afraid they would see inside of her if they looked for too long a time, but they definitely were welcome to look long enough to see how beautiful she was.

She went downstairs and joined the family in the living room. "Would anyone care for some coffee or something to eat?" she asked. They were all looking oddly at her. She glanced at Carter, but he seemed preoccupied, like he was staring through her even though his eyes were focused on her. She felt self-conscious. "Carter?"

He blinked. "Oh. No thanks, hon. We're all set," he answered slowly.

Morgan tensed. "Is something wrong?" she asked in a low voice.

"No, honey. Everything's fine," Carter answered with a tight smile.

Hunter stood up. "I'd better be going. I have to finish packing. I'm leaving this weekend."

"We'll miss you, Hunter," Paul stated.

"Everyone's welcome to visit whenever you can get away."

"We'll definitely plan a trip to California," Sarah said.

"Let me know if you need help with anything, Hunter," Carter offered.

Hunter looked at him, opened his mouth as though he were about to say something, then as if in an afterthought, firmly clamped it shut.

"You'd better keep in touch," Collin ordered.

"I will." He turned his attention to Morgan.

Morgan flashed him a warm, friendly smile.   "   I wish you and the kids only the best, Hunter."

He frowned. "I trust there won't be any more deaths in the family."

"I'm going to put some coffee on," Morgan mumbled, hurrying from the room.

Carter gritted his teeth. "Hunter, please don't make accusations you can't prove."

Hunter squinted. "What are you going to say, Carter, if it's proven? If I'm right, how will you feel then?"

****

Carter lay in bed, tossing and turning for hours. He pleaded for sleep to come, but it only eluded him. His family's suspicions of Morgan tormented him. He stole a glance at her, lying in a peaceful slumber next to him. He tenderly ran his fingertips over her smooth cheek. She stirred briefly but didn't awaken. He put his arms behind his head and stared at the ceiling. He had to prove his family wrong. But how? Morgan's lack of a past didn't help her cause, at least not where his family was concerned. And he was ashamed to admit that at times he wondered about her himself. He tried several times to get her to tell him something, anything about

183

her past, but she adamantly refused. He assumed whatever was back there was too painful for her to talk about and had always closed the topic rather than cause her pain. Maybe someday she would feel secure and confident enough in his love to open up to him. He would help her through whatever demons resided in her past.

Raindrops splattered gently against the windowpane of the open window. Carter breathed deeply. He loved the smell of rain, always had ever since he was a young boy. The room lit up with a bright flash of lightning, rapidly followed by an ear-shattering clap of thunder. He listened to the steady rhythm of the rain and his eyes grew heavy with sleep. Like a mother singing a lullaby to her restless child, the rain calmed his restless mind and soon he drifted off into a deep slumber.

****

Sheriff Birch rapped lightly on Carter's office door.

"Come on in," Carter called from the other side.

Jake Birch and Mark Barlow made their way into the newly remodeled office.

Carter looked up from a blueprint. "What can I do for you?" he asked, peering at them.

"First off, Carter, I want to offer my condolences on the loss of your sister. Payton was a fine young woman and I'm shocked at the circumstances surrounding her death," Jake said.

"Thank you." Carter removed his reading glasses. "It's been rough. The family's still in town. They'll be leaving in a day or so." He nodded to his desk. "I stole away for a couple of hours to get some work done. I need to keep busy."

"I understand," Jake said.

"Do you have any news? About Payton's death or my mother's?"

Jake shifted uncomfortably from one foot to the other. "No, nothing yet." He glanced around the office. "I didn't expect to see you here this morning," he said, seating himself in a large leather chair. Mark sat in a high-backed wooden chair.

"I wouldn't have come in, but keeping busy helps me to get through each day." He looked intently at them. "So if you have no news about the murders, why are you here?"

"I'll get straight to the point, Carter."

"I wish you would, Sheriff," Carter said coldly.

"What do you know about your wife's background?"

"Why is everyone so damned intent on blaming my wife? I'll prove you all wrong! She's not a murderer!" he shouted, pounding his fist on his desk.

Jake observed him cautiously. He'd never known Carter to show such an outburst before. "No one has accused her of anything," Jake said. "All I asked is what do you know about her background?"

"All I need to know. I don't have to answer any of your questions, Sheriff," Carter replied, eyeing him sharply. "I suggest you both leave my office now. If this continues, I'll file a suit against you for harassment!"

Jake's voice softened. "Please, Carter. For your own sake talk to me."

Carter rubbed his jaw. "Okay, you want some answers," he bellowed. "I'll answer your questions and then you stay the hell away from me and my family!"

"Fair enough." Jake glanced at Mark.

185

Mark sat carefully observing Carter's reactions. He nodded to Jake.

"Tell me everything you know about Morgan."

"There's really not much to tell," he said coldly. "No trail of dead bodies in her past if that's what you're looking for. She comes from a large family with whom she never got along and broke off all contact with them years ago. I don't bring it up because it's very painful for her. She didn't have a happy childhood."

"We've checked into her background," Jake stated.

"And?" Carter asked sarcastically.

He nodded toward Mark. "I'll let Investigator Barlow give you the information."

Mark Barlow pulled a notebook from his jacket pocket. He flipped slowly through it. "I contacted Morgan's father," he began. "According to him, it appears that during Morgan's teenage years she started exhibiting delusional ideas and thoughts."

"What did he do about it?"

"He sought help at a mental health clinic, and for a while she seemed as though she was getting better, but she became very possessive of what she thought was hers. She wouldn't allow anyone to come between her and whomever or whatever happened to be the object of her attention."

"Her father could be lying possibly to cover his abuse of her."

Mark shook his head. "I don't think so, Carter."

"Something must've happened in her childhood then to cause her to react possessively," he reasoned.

Mark flipped to another page. "Her father admits that

he was a strict disciplinarian."

"Can I assume his parenting skills would be called child abuse in today's terminology?" Carter asked.

"I think that's being presumptuous."

"Like making false accusations against my wife?"

"Has Morgan told you about any of her past relationships?"

"No, I never asked because I don't care. That's in the past and has no bearing on my relationship with her today."

Mark cleared his throat. "During her teen years she dated one boy in particular for quite a length of time. On three separate occasions this boy tried to end the relationship, but she would cry and carry on and threaten to commit suicide so he would stay with her."

Carter shrugged his shoulders. "That doesn't prove anything. Teens are always falling in and out of love. The teenage years can be intense when it comes to love," he said. "We've all been there."

"That's very true, but in Morgan's case it was different. She was extremely possessive of the boy. He was close to his sister, which tortured Morgan. She couldn't bear the thought of him caring for anyone but her." Mark studied Carter's reaction to his words. He sensed that what he was saying was beginning to sink in.

Carter rubbed his chin. "Would you like some coffee?"

Before they could answer, he had already poured three cups. He needed a few minutes to collect his thoughts. Morgan could be possessive, but he assumed most women were like that. If he even casually glanced at a woman passing on the street, it would upset her terribly and he'd have to spend hours assuring her that she was the only woman he ever wanted. No. They were messing with his head. No one knew Morgan like he did. She could never harm another human being. She didn't have it in her.

He handed the men the steaming cups of coffee. "Well, obviously she and the boy finally parted ways or I wouldn't be with her now."

"It wasn't as smooth as that," Mark replied.

Carter raised his eyebrows. "So, what happened?"

Mark took a deep breath. "The boy's sister had a terrible accident. Both of her legs and one of her arms were broken."

Carter's eyebrows knitted together. "And she accused Morgan?"

"Morgan invited the girl over to spend the evening. They went up to the attic to look through old trunks. On the way back down the stairs, the girl apparently tripped. She was questioned thoroughly and she repeatedly said that she tripped on something lying on the stairs. It wasn't until years later that she finally admitted Morgan pushed her." He eyed Carter closely.

"Why didn't the girl tell then and there if Morgan had pushed her?" he said, unconvinced. "That doesn't make sense. Why would she wait? Sounds fishy to me."

"Morgan threatened to kill her if she ever told anyone the truth about what really happened that night."

Carter chuckled. "And you believe her? The girl could be lying." He lifted an eyebrow. "This is ludicrous."

"I talked to her, Carter," Mark Barlow stated.

He shook his head back and forth. "This is unbelievable,"

he muttered. "Why are you out to pin this on my wife?"

"Carter," Jake said quietly, "I've known you all your life. You know I'd never do anything to intentionally hurt you or your family."

Carter's eyes narrowed. "Whatever happened to the boy?" he asked Barlow. He took a swallow of coffee.

"He died."

Carter almost choked on his coffee. He coughed and then cleared his throat. "How?"

"He was poisoned," Barlow answered. "His death was listed as a suicide, but many suspected otherwise. Unfortunately there was never enough evidence to charge Morgan with any crime."

"Why would she have been a suspect? If she loved him that much, why would she kill him?" Carter's insides felt like they were freezing up.

"Because she didn't want anyone else to have him if she couldn't. She was the last person to see him alive. He'd agreed to meet her at a café. Supposedly, she wanted to talk things out to have some kind of closure. He'd told his family about it and they tried to convince him not to meet with her, but he insisted that this would be the end of her meddling in his life." Mark paused. "Somehow she slipped something into his coffee. He came home, went to bed, and never woke up. An autopsy was performed, which showed a lethal dose of slow-acting poison in his system."

"That still doesn't prove it was her. If it was she would have been charged with murder." Carter swallowed hard. "You said yourself there wasn't enough evidence to charge her."

"Carter, Emily's death never made sense to me," Jake explained. "A poor swimmer doesn't just decide to dive off a raft to impress someone she asked to give her swimming lessons."

Carter's shoulders slumped. "No," he said hoarsely. He looked into Jake's eyes. "I can't believe she would be capable of anything like that. No one knows her like I do."

"What about her friends? Has she ever talked about anyone from her past? Or been in contact with friends?"

"No. She's always been a loner," he confided.

"Didn't you find that strange?" Mark asked.

Carter emphatically shook his head. "No. Why should it? People get busy with their lives and friendships sometimes fall by the wayside."

"But they usually have someone. Especially since she comes from such a large family."

"Not if they've been mistreated by their family." Carter's head began to ache. He needed to process everything he was being told. He didn't want to believe any of it, but the truth was he had doubted what she'd said about Emily's drowning. But then again, she might have been confused since she'd just witnessed a drowning. He didn't know what to believe. All he knew was that three members of his family were dead.

"She needs help, Carter," Jake said quietly.

"But we still don't know that she's done anything wrong." He stood up. "No, I don't want to hear anymore. Why is everyone ganging up on her?" he demanded. "When you can give me concrete proof that she's committed a crime, then I'll listen, but not until then."

"Weldon doesn't need any more murders, Carter, and neither does your family."

"Then go find the person who murdered my mother and sister."

Mark ran his hand through his hair. "Carter, please work with us. Maybe it's just a hunch, but I feel it in every fiber of my being." He threw his hands up. "Look, if we're wrong, then I'll publicly admit it and give you and Morgan an apology. That'll clear anyone's suspicions of her, and Jake and I will leave her alone. You have nothing to lose here, Carter."

Carter frowned. "Okay, but when we find out that everything she's been accused of is unfounded, I'll expect that public apology."

"You've got it," Mark said.

"I still think that Morgan's father is lying when he said Morgan is mentally ill. He could be lying to protect himself for abusing his children," Carter said weakly.

"I talked to several people, Carter. Including her siblings. Her father was not abusive," Mark said.

"She doesn't have a mean bone in her body," Carter insisted. "I've known her long enough that I would have seen that side of her."

"Sometimes we don't want to see what's right in front of us."

Carter thought about what his mother and Payton had told him about Morgan. He'd taken his wife's side as any decent husband would do. Could Morgan have really been treating them the way they said she had? Now they were both dead. Suddenly he brightened. She couldn't be responsible for what had happened at Payton's apartment. She had proof that she'd been at the art show. Her parking pass was stamped. Whoever had left the message for Payton had also cut her brake line.

"Everyone I talked to had the same story to tell," Barlow continued. "Anyone she cared about became a possession to her, and heaven help the person who tried to take what she believed was hers."

"Why haven't her parents or family ever tried to contact her all these years?" Carter asked.

"Her father doesn't ever want to see her again. In his mind, she dead." He let his breath out slowly. "Her mother agrees. And that has to be a difficult decision to come to regarding your own child."

"What about her brothers and sisters?"

"They've gone on with their lives, and as far as they're concerned, don't have room for her in their lives."

Carter paced back and forth. "But if she was abused, that wasn't right either."

"No, it wasn't." Mark stared at him. "If she really was abused."

Carter nervously ran his hand through his hair. "I don't know what to think."

"Keep a close eye on her," Mark said.

"I don't want her to think that I believe she's guilty of anything, because I sincerely don't. It will take more than what you've told me to convince me."

Mark flipped through some more pages in his notebook. "From the scenario that Jake and I have constructed, we've concluded that Morgan has set a pattern. We believe she's out to destroy the members of your family whom she believes pose a threat to her security. How does Morgan get along with your brothers and their wives?"

"She has a friendly relationship with Collin and Jude. In fact, we spent the weekend with them not long ago."

"How'd that go?" Mark asked.

"We had an enjoyable time."

"What about Paul and his wife?" Jake asked.

"She gets along well with Paul, but she's not overly fond of Sarah. But then Sarah has never been easy to get along with. She's nice enough but is a hypochondriac."

"How's Paul's restaurant doing? They live in Vermont, don't they?" Jake asked.

"Yes, it's doing very well from what Paul says."

"Are you planning any visits to Vermont in the near future?"

"As a matter of fact we're planning to spend Labor Day weekend with them."

"Whose idea was it for the visit?" Mark asked.

"Does it matter?" Carter looked at him.

"It could."

"Morgan's." He eyed them suspiciously. "I know what you're thinking. Morgan is trying to get along better with everyone in the family. She's been making the effort."

"Wasn't it also her idea to go to Portland to visit Payton?"

He shook his head. "No, she wanted to go to the art festival. Since Payton lived in Portland it made sense for us to stay with her."

"Sarah could be the next person on Morgan's list," Mark reasoned.

Carter laughed bitterly. "I don't think she has a list."

"Just keep an eye on your wife. You might be surprised what you'll find out."

Carter distractedly tapped a pencil on his desk. "I don't like snooping on my wife. If she ever found out, she'd never forgive me, and I wouldn't blame her. What is she supposed to think if her own husband doesn't trust her?" He eyed them cautiously. "But I'll go along with you just to prove my wife's innocence once and for all. Then I want the accusations against her put to rest. All you've given me are unfounded bits of information. If you can prove what you've said, that'll be a different story." His jaw tightened. "But when you're proven wrong, I'll expect the public apology to my wife and me as you've promised."

Jake shifted in his seat. "Carter, I know we're asking a lot of you, and I understand how you feel. But we need your help on this one. Morgan won't find out, I promise you. We'll put the authorities in Vermont on notice."

"I hope, for your sake, that she is innocent, Carter. I sincerely do," Mark said.

Carter looked closely at both men. "You know you're both going to feel like fools when this is over, don't you? I'm only going along with it to get you off our backs. That doesn't mean I believe a word you've said." He stood up. "Now if you'll excuse me, I have some paperwork to catch up on."

Carter held the door for them, and after they left, sat back down at his desk. His mind whirled with what-ifs. How well did he really know Morgan? He was ashamed to admit the doubts he had about her secretive past. Was there any truth to the story about the boy and his sister? Maybe her father had done something far worse to her and made up stories to protect himself. He shook his head. What Barlow said about Morgan's possessiveness made him wonder. She was possessive and he'd always known that. He wondered if Becca was just another one of her possessions. He wanted his daughter to have a happy, secure upbringing and enter her adult years as a well-adjusted woman, able to face the challenges that would await her. He knew deep in his heart that Morgan would never harm Becca for anything, so he wouldn't concern himself with suppositions in that matter. His own hidden suspicions about his wife made him sick to his stomach. He felt like he was betraying her.

He put his head between his hands and let the hot, heavy tears of frustration fall. He loved her so deeply. He had to prove everyone wrong. Morgan was the woman he wanted to grow old with. Jake and Barlow were causing him to have doubts about his wife, but he would fight those doubts. Morgan needed him even more than she realized, and he would never let her know what he was about to do.

He blew his nose and pulled himself together. He had to be careful and act naturally around her. She would be justifiably hurt if she even suspected his plan to go along with Barlow and Birch. Even though he was only doing it to get them off her back once and for all, he instinctively knew that she just wouldn't understand.

CHAPTER FOURTEEN

Morgan finished dusting the coffee table. "Would you like some more coffee, Jude?" she offered hospitably.

"No, thanks," Jude answered as she stared distractedly out of the window.

Morgan turned her attention to Collin and Paul, who were in the middle of a heated card game while Sarah was patiently teaching Raine how to crochet. She would've offered them refreshments but didn't want to intrude upon them. She walked over to her daughter, and then bent down to her. Becca giggled and pulled the dust cloth from Morgan's hand. Morgan laughed as Becca wobbled over to the coffee table and swished the cloth over it. She left Becca to her task and joined Jude by the window. "Looks like rain," she observed, seeing the black clouds in the distance. "Hope we don't get a bad storm."

"Oh, I'm sure the garden will appreciate the rain," Jude said.

"Well, we still have plenty of good weather ahead of us."

"With everything that's happened this spring and

summer, I don't think anyone's cared much about whether the sun shines or not this year," Jude answered sadly.

Morgan shrugged. "But we have to go on living," she said softly.

"It's hard sometimes." Jude turned to Morgan. "I'm scared. Don't you ever get frightened? Don't you wonder who's doing this to our family?"

She nodded. "Yes, Jude, I do, but if I dwell on it, it only drives me crazy with fear. I'm trying to cope like everyone else, and keeping to my normal routine helps me get through it."

"I suppose that's the best way," she said wistfully. "But I still wish we could turn back time and that we would find this to be just some horrible nightmare."

Morgan patted her hand. "Let me make you a nice cup of tea. That'll make you feel better."

Jude smiled. "Thank you, Morgan."

****

Morgan snuggled close to Carter. "Are you tired, honey?"

He put an arm around her, drawing her closer to him. "What do you have in mind?" he whispered.

She squeezed his arm affectionately. "I just want to talk."

He ran his fingertips over her arm. "Okay. Is there anything in particular you want to discuss?"

She sighed. "I just wish I could get closer to your family. I've tried, but I don't think they'll ever accept me." She drew a deep breath. "I hope they don't believe what Hunter's been saying."

"I don't think most of them do," Carter replied. "You've always gotten along well with Jude and Raine. They certainly don't believe a word he's said."

"Jude acts different around me. She's not as talkative as she used to be."

"Don't worry about what anyone thinks of you. All that matters is how I feel about you, honey." He kissed the top of her head. "Can I ask you a question?"

"Of course."

"You've never told me much about your past." Carter doubted she'd tell him much, if anything, but he needed to hear the truth from her own lips about what happened to the boy and his sister Mark Barlow had told him about. The problem was finding a way to lead into it. In his heart he'd never doubt her and felt ashamed when he let others plant the seeds of doubt. If he'd had a horrible childhood, as he assumed she had, he wouldn't want to talk about it either. That also could be why she had no close friends. She had a trust issue and he couldn't hold that against her.

She stiffened. "I've told you everything you need to know."

"There is so much more I want to know about you instead of the bare bones condensed version you gave me. Someday Becca is going to want to know the family history of both her parents."

"Why are you asking me now after all this time?"

He sighed. "I told you...for Becca. If anything were to happen to either of us she would know nothing about your side of the family, but she'd have enough material from my side to fill a library."

"She'll be better off forgetting all about my side of the family," she said curtly.

This was not going the way Carter had hoped. Feeling her body snuggled close to him convinced him even further that she didn't have a violent bone in her body. He almost laughed out loud picturing her building a bomb and cutting brake lines. It only proved to him that Sheriff Birch and Mark Barlow were desperate to pin the murders on someone. He decided to just dive in with his questions. "Did you have many boyfriends?"

She inhaled sharply. "Why are you asking me these questions, Carter? I've told you over and over that I don't get along with my family and that I dated a few boys, but none were special enough to keep me there."

"Come on," he prodded. "There wasn't any one special boy that maybe you could've been persuaded to stick around for?"

"No, there was no one."

He lay back staring at the ceiling. She wasn't going to budge. He decided to try another tactic...maybe that would get her to open up. "I remember my first love." He sighed. He felt her tense up.

"Do you still think about her?" she asked tonelessly.

"That was years ago."

"Does she still live in Weldon?"

"No, her family moved when we were juniors in high school."

"If she hadn't moved away then maybe you'd have married her."

"But she did move. Even though at the time I didn't

think I would survive, I did." He shifted. "You never had a boyfriend who made you feel that way?" he persisted.

"No, Carter, I've never cared about anyone the way I do you. When I met you, I put my past behind me and concentrated only on the future. The past is dead and gone." She yawned. "I'm tired. I want to go to sleep now."

****

Jake and Mark sat in a booth at Nora's, large bowls of fish chowder in front of them.

"Nora makes the best chowder in New England," Jake boasted.

"It's delicious," Mark agreed.

Jake wiped his mouth on his napkin. "Ahh," he said, sighing contentedly. "Boston going to let you stay for a while?"

"They want this wrapped up as badly as you do." Mark sipped at his iced tea. "Do you think Carter will tell us if his wife says anything suspicious?"

"That's hard to say. He said he's tried to question her about her past, but she clams up. He'll never be convinced that she's done anything wrong. I just wish there was some proof beyond a shadow of a doubt."

Mark frowned. "She's going to slip up. They always do."

"I hope it's before she claims another victim. She's sly, no doubt about it," Jake said, wondering if they ever would be able to trap her.

"It makes you wonder what she's thinking when she commits the murders." Mark looked intently at him.

Jake shuddered. "It makes me wonder if she even has

a heart because she certainly has no conscience."

Mark was thoughtful for a minute. "I wish I could get inside her mind to see how she truly operates."

Jake chuckled. "I'd be scared shitless if I knew what was really going through her mind."

He threw a few bills on the table. "I guess we'd better get back over to your office and go over everything one more time."

"What are we not seeing?" Jake rubbed his tired eyes. "We haven't missed a thing, Mark."

"There's got to be something," Barlow answered with determination. "I won't rest until I find the one thing that'll prove she's guilty."

****

Carter wished Morgan would open up about her past. He surely would understand anything she told him. He wanted to help her fight the demons from her past, but she put up a wall where anything before she met him existed. He wanted—no, he desperately *needed*—to prove her innocence. He wished he could just come right out and tell her why he was questioning her.

He looked through the neatly organized closets in the master bedroom. Everything was as it should be. She hadn't held on to even one memento from her past. Not even a high school yearbook. How odd, he thought, that she wouldn't have kept even a book or favorite doll, but there was nothing. He felt guilty sneaking around, looking for what he didn't even know. He'd practically pushed Morgan and Becca out the door to go grocery shopping. His family had left at the crack of dawn for their own homes.

201

This was the only opportunity he might have to see if Morgan had any hidden evidence. He laughed at his own absurd thoughts. He didn't know what he expected to find. A book on bomb-making or how to cut a brake line? He laid on the floor and looked under the bed. Nothing. Not even a dust bunny. But that was due to Morgan's immaculate house cleaning. Everything was always spotless. Sometimes he thought she was too neat and tidy. She was always there with a dust cloth the minute Becca's little fingerprints showed up on the coffee table. Sometimes he wished she'd lighten up just a little.

He pulled himself to a sitting position and leaned his back against the bureau. He hated the seeds of doubt Mark Barlow and Jake Birch had planted in his mind. They had no right. He wouldn't crack under their pressure. Once he told them there was nothing to be found, he'd also tell them he would be seeking legal representation if their accusations continued. It wasn't right to destroy someone's reputation from comments made years ago. They'd already decided to believe Morgan's family. That pissed him off. If they wanted war, he'd give it to them. After today he was done. They'd either leave his family alone or face the consequences.

He placed his hands on the floor to raise himself when his eyes settled on something shiny from under the nightstand across the room. He hurried over to the nightstand and bent down, reaching his hand underneath. He pulled out a small metal box. He stared at it for a few seconds. He wondered how long the box had been there. Maybe Morgan did have a special box she kept special treasures in. He wanted to look inside, but did he have the right? That would be violating her personal space. But then again, maybe there was something inside the box that would prove her innocence. But if she found out he'd been snooping into her personal items, she'd never forgive him. He sat for a few minutes debating what to do. He had to make a decision quickly or she'd come home and he may never get another chance.

He needed to open it. With shaky hands, he tried to open it but found it locked. He looked through Morgan's nightstand drawer and then her jewelry box in search of the key, but came up empty. Morgan probably had the key with her. He studied the lock. It was a cheap box and the lock looked relatively easy to pick. He sifted once again through the nightstand, finally finding a paperclip, which he bent and twisted. He maneuvered the clip into the lock. It took a few minutes of manipulating it before the lock popped open. Once again his conscience kicked in telling him he had no right to open the box. No, he had to know what secrets the box held. The clue to the past his wife couldn't bring herself to talk about probably lay inside.

He drew a deep breath, filled his lungs, then slowly exhaled. He opened the box and peered inside. An assortment of items filled the box. A picture of a teenage boy sitting on top smiled up at him. Carter studied the picture for a few minutes. The boy was extremely handsome with curly jet black hair. His eyes twinkled mischievously. Carter wondered if this was the same boy Barlow had told him about. He turned the picture over. Nothing was scrawled on the back...no name or date. He set the picture back into the box, and then sifted through the other items. He saw the love letters the boy had written to her when they were dating. He smiled. She was normal after all. The boy must have meant a great deal to her for her to keep the letters. He assumed the breakup was bad and that's why she didn't want to talk about it. Relief swept through him and his nerves calmed down.

A folded sheet of paper caught his attention. He carefully unfolded it and looked at it. His hands shook and his chest constricted. "Oh my God," he moaned. "No, Morgan. I won't believe this." He stuffed the paper back into the box, in the exact spot he had found it, and then closed the lid making certain the box was locked. He quickly shoved it back under the nightstand.

He had to pull himself together before Morgan came back. He walked downstairs to his den and uncharacteristically poured himself a double shot of whiskey. He gulped it down. It didn't help so he poured another. He stood by the window, staring at Morgan's vegetable garden. How patient she was with her garden, he thought. She'd spend hours pulling weeds and hoeing, enjoying every minute of it. When she was in her garden she was at peace.

He sat down at his desk, trying to make sense out of what he had seen written on that paper. There had to be some kind of explanation. Maybe she was keeping a record, he reasoned. But why would she write "Completed" next to the names of the deceased members of his family? Maybe she meant that their time on this earth was completed, he rationalized. The piece of paper wasn't evidence that she'd done anything wrong. He decided not to tell Mark or Jake about it. They would run off half-cocked, and God only knew what those two would do to her. He'd keep this information to himself.

CHAPTER FIFTEEN

The days dragged on hot and heavy, and Weldon slowly returned to normal as summer neared its end. As each day passed, people talked less and less about the murders. It appeared that the Rogers' family streak of deaths had ended. Carter threw himself into his work, and Morgan busied herself, as usual, with Becca, the house, and her beloved garden. Mark Barlow had even returned to Boston. The investigation appeared to be over. Carter resigned himself to the fact that the murders of his mother and sister would never be solved. They'd end up as cold cases. He had to accept it and move on with his life. Now that Jake and Mark were no longer hounding him, it would be easier to do.

Carter looked at the picture of Morgan adorning his desk. She was beautiful, and he was lucky to have her. No one saw the side of Morgan he understood and loved. Just because every detail of her life wasn't public knowledge, she would always be an outsider. It didn't matter if she lived here for the next fifty years. It wouldn't change. In conversations with his family, they too, seemed to be settling back into the routines of their daily lives. None of them mentioned Morgan's name in connection to any of the deaths, and if any one of them believed she played a part, it wasn't mentioned to him.

Morgan's garden flourished under her care. The fruits of her labor were paying off, and every evening Carter was pleasantly surprised to see what adorned his dinner table. He'd put the paper he'd seen from her metal box out of his mind. Morgan was cheerful during the day, and warm and loving through the dark hours of the night. He couldn't help but find himself falling even deeper in love with his wife.

Carter walked through the dark, silent rooms of his home. Morgan had gone to bed hours ago. He went up with her, but when sleep refused to come, he silently stole back downstairs. He walked back into his den and turned on the light, then moved to his desk and again picked up the picture of Morgan. She smiled seductively at him. He remembered when he took the picture two years earlier. He'd taken several pictures of her that day. It had been a hot, lazy afternoon and they'd spent the entire day together doing nothing but enjoying one another's company. After he took this picture, they'd climbed into bed and spent the rest of the afternoon making love.

An hour later, he tiptoed upstairs and quietly slipped into Becca's room. For twenty minutes, he stood at the head of her crib, staring down at her. She looked like a slumbering princess. He bent down and kissed her cheek. She stirred slightly as a smiled traced her lips.

He smiled as he left the room, closing the door softly behind himself. He walked into his bedroom and wearily climbed back into bed. Almost instantly, Morgan maneuvered herself snugly against him. He sighed contentedly, then kissed her shoulder and stroked her hair. They would be leaving for Vermont tomorrow, and this trip would prove once and for all that Morgan was innocent.

****

He woke at seven, rubbing the sleep from his eyes. He wondered why he had such trouble falling asleep, and just when it seemed he was finally resting comfortably, it was time to awaken. He yawned and turned toward Morgan. She was sleeping peacefully. He hurriedly threw his clothes on, and then silently slipped out of the house. He needed to finish up some paperwork before they left for Paul and Sarah's.

Morgan had breakfast on the table when he returned. Becca was sitting in her high chair, eating a bowl of corn flakes, milk dripping down her chin.

"Hi, honey," Morgan said brightly. "Where have you been?" She kissed his cheek.

"I had to clear up a few things at the office. What's for breakfast?"

"Your favorite," she beamed. "Pancakes."

"Great!" he exclaimed enthusiastically. "But you really shouldn't have gone to all this trouble."

"Nothing's too good for my husband." She lovingly put her arms around his neck. He felt the stirring of desire rise within him.

"Keep this up and we'll be skipping breakfast," he warned as he patted her butt. She laughingly tempted him with a huge stack of pancakes. "On second thought, pass the syrup," he joked.

When they finished eating, Morgan cleared the table, and then loaded the dishwasher while Carter took Becca outside to play. She poured herself a second cup of coffee. She was agitated. The last time she'd opened her metal box, she found some of the items askew. She wondered if Carter had gotten into the box. If he had, had he seen the paper? But if he had, why hadn't he said anything to her about it? She distractedly picked at a fingernail. He would've said something, wouldn't he? *No, I'm wrong*, she finally convinced her tormented mind. Maybe I was in a hurry the last time I opened the box.

She finished her coffee, then walked upstairs into her bedroom. She peered out of the window, gazing down upon Carter and Becca. They sat across from one another on the lawn, rolling a large ball back and forth. She walked to her closet and removed several cartons stored in the back. She had to half-crawl into the back to find the shoebox tucked securely out of view on a shelf hidden by her many dresses. She tore the lid from the box and reached inside to pull out a small handgun. She lovingly cradled the weapon in her hands. The gun could never be traced back to her. The man in Dorchester assured her of it. She hated that horrible street, but it served its purpose, as everything eventually serves its purpose.

She laid the gun back in the box, carefully tucking tissue around it. She took her overnight bag from the closet and placed the shoebox securely inside. She added her cosmetics, toiletries, and a few undergarments, and then snapped the case shut and locked it. She double-checked the case and set it aside. Next, she took a large suitcase from the closet and packed the necessary clothes for her and Carter. She walked into Becca's room and packed two large bags, then carried the bags downstairs. She set them at the bottom of the stairs and then returned to her room for her suitcase and overnight bag. She set them next to the bags and rounded up her husband and daughter.

Carter glanced at his wristwatch. "It's only eleven o'clock. I hadn't planned to leave until noon."

"What difference will an hour make? We can stop somewhere for lunch. If we have lunch here, then we won't be on the road until one by the time I clean up," she reasoned.

"You're right," he agreed. He picked up the suitcases and bags and carried them out to the car. After he placed them inside, he entered the kitchen and poured a glass of water. "Are the windows and front door locked?"

"Yes, I took care of everything." Morgan smiled.

"Okay. I'm going to put on a pair of shorts. It's going to be a scorcher today."

"Okay, honey."

"Mama…coo-kie!" Becca begged.

Morgan laughed. "All right, honey, Mama will give you a cookie." She grabbed one from the cookie jar on the counter. Becca excitedly snatched the homemade sugar cookie from her mother's hand and then plopped down on the kitchen floor.

Carter returned clad in an old pair of cutoff jean shorts and a pale blue T-shirt. "I'm ready," he announced.

"Good," Morgan answered, picking Becca up off the floor. "Here, Daddy," she cooed as she handed Carter their child.

Moments later Carter slowly backed the car down the driveway. "Where are my sunglasses?" he asked.

Morgan took them out of the glove box and handed

them to him. "Where you always leave them, honey," she said, grinning. She turned on the radio, settled back into her seat, and watched the scenery whiz by. She closed her eyes and soon drifted off into a semiconscious state. When she opened her eyes again, the car had stopped at a fast food restaurant. Carter had Becca's hand firmly in his and they both were staring at her.

"Well hello, sleepyhead." He chuckled. Becca looked at her father, and then imitated his laughter.

"What time is it?" she asked as she stretched her aching body.

"About two o'clock. Did you have a good rest?"

"I did."

"Well, come on! Becca and I are starved!"

She laughed as she climbed out of the car.

****

After their quick lunch, Morgan prompted Carter to allow her to take over the driving.

"I don't know, honey. There's too much traffic today."

"When isn't there traffic?"

He hesitated. "All right, but please watch your speed," he cautioned.

Morgan backed out of the parking lot, sideswiping a van as she made her exit. Carter cringed but said nothing.

"Did you see that guy?" she asked, turning to him.

"Just keep your eyes on the road, honey," Carter insisted. He'd be on edge for the rest of the trip. It was difficult to relax with Morgan behind the wheel. It wasn't that she was a terrible driver; he just didn't think she had the patience to be a driver period.

210

"We're almost there," Morgan triumphantly announced an hour later.

Carter breathed a sigh of relief. "I'm glad we made it in one piece!"

"I can't wait to see the remodeling they've done to the house and restaurant," she said.

Becca smiled and clapped her hands when Terence and Lisa picked her up out of her car seat and carried her into the house. Morgan and Carter trailed behind. Sarah and Paul met them at the door.

"Come on in!" Paul exuberantly greeted them, grabbing the suitcases from Carter's hands. "I've got a pitcher of cool drinks waiting."

Sarah led them into the living room. "What do you think?" she boasted proudly.

Morgan eyed Sarah's collection of antiques. "It must've taken you forever to collect these pieces, Sarah!" Morgan exclaimed. Her eyes traveled around the living room. "This room is beautiful."

"Thank you," Sarah answered.

Paul threw an arm around his wife. "Sarah has a unique gift for decorating. I told her she should be an interior decorator."

"She certainly has a knack for it," Carter agreed. He looked around the room. "I like the size of it, Paul. Not too big and not too small. It's perfect."

"It was tiny before we knocked down the wall by the entrance hall," he explained. "We thought we were getting in over our heads, but everything fell into place."

"It was difficult dealing with the construction," Sarah

said. "It was a complete mess!"

Paul affectionately squeezed her shoulder. "Yes, but it was worth it, because now we have the home just the way we envisioned it."

"We do," she agreed. "Would anyone care for a drink?"

"I've got to get the baby ready for bed," Morgan said. "Maybe after I get her settled."

"We've set up a crib in the room you and Carter will be staying in. I'll show you the way," Sarah said.

Morgan scooped Becca into her arms and followed Sarah up the enormous staircase.

Paul turned to Carter. "What took you so long to get here? Traffic bad? We expected you a couple of hours ago. Sarah was beginning to worry."

"We would've been here before this, but Morgan spied a couple of shops…you know how she is when she gets into an antiques shop."

He laughed. "Did she find any interesting treasures?"

"She did, but I didn't."

Paul laughed again. "I know the feeling. Sarah's the same way, as you can tell by her vast collection." His attention turned to shouting coming from the corner of the room. "Terence and Lisa, it's about time you two got ready for bed," he ordered.

"Aw, Dad, can't we stay up just a little longer tonight?" they protested in unison.

"Upstairs, now," he said firmly.

They looked at him with sad faces, and when they saw he wasn't about to change his mind, reluctantly left the room.

Paul handed Carter a drink. "I've got a babysitter

coming at nine o'clock. Is that all right? I thought the four of us could have dinner in the restaurant…that is, if you're not too tired from the drive." He looked hopefully at Carter.

"No, that sounds great. I'm sure Morgan will agree," he replied. "Besides, I can't wait to see what you've done over there."

He smiled. "Good. Maybe you'd better let Morgan know."

"You're right. It'll take her an hour to get dressed," he said with a wink.

Paul grinned. "I've got one of those, too."

****

An hour later, the two couples were seated around a table, sipping cocktails in Paul and Sarah's restaurant.

"This is beautiful!" Morgan said. "I can't believe it's the same place."

"It took a lot of time and more money than I cared to part with, but I think it'll pay for itself in the long run," Paul bragged.

Morgan admired the decor. Several old and valuable paintings adorned the walls. A dimly lit light cast a glow over each painting. Her eye caught a picture of Boston Harbor. The light dancing on the water made her feel as though she were at the harbor at that exact moment in time. She liked the way the many nautical artifacts were displayed throughout the room. The tables and chairs were Early American and each table was covered with a delicate cloth. The room could easily seat two hundred people, and Paul let them know there were four more rooms individually decorated for banquets and receptions. They were already booked up for the holidays.

Morgan found the atmosphere of the room casual and relaxing.

"Business must be good, then" Carter remarked at the rapidly filling tables.

"It's been fantastic!" Sarah said excitedly. "You usually need a reservation to get in, and we have people booked for weeks from now. The kitchen doesn't close until midnight, unlike most places that close at ten."

"That explains why so many people are still coming in." Carter smiled at her. "It looks like you've finally gotten what you've dreamed of."

Paul squeezed his wife's hand. "It was our teamwork," he said. "We couldn't have done any of it without the support of each other."

A waiter arrived at their table. "I can take your order if you're ready, Mr. Rogers."

Paul looked at the others. "I think we're ready." He glanced at his wife. "Sarah, would you like to start?"

"I'll have lobster," she answered.

"Lobster sounds good," Carter said.

Morgan nodded in agreement.

"Make it four lobsters," Paul instructed. He topped it off with a bottle of wine. "Have you heard from Hunter?" he asked after the waiter left.

"He called a couple of weeks ago. He sounded better. Says the kids are adjusting very well to the move."

"Do you think he's adjusting, Carter?"

Carter frowned. "He sounded cheerful enough, but I guess it's going to take a long time before we see the old Hunter again. I can't imagine what he's going through without Emily." An unnoticeable shudder ran through him as he looked at Morgan. The flickering light from the candle sitting in the middle of the table illuminated her beautiful face, and Carter was swept away as he always was when he gazed at her. He reached for her hand under the table. When his hand touched hers, she looked into his eyes and love for her flooded through him.

When their meals arrived, they ate slowly, making small talk. During coffee, Carter tried unsuccessfully to stifle a yawn.

"You look tired, Carter," Paul said.

"I am," he admitted. "But nothing a good night's sleep won't cure."

"Well, I've got a full day planned for us tomorrow," Paul announced. "So if everyone's ready..." He stood up.

Twenty minutes later, they were back at Paul and Sarah's house. "It's a beautiful night," Paul noted getting out of the car.

"Too good to waste on sleep," Morgan announced. "I'd like to go for a walk."

"I'll go with you," Sarah offered.

Carter stiffened, and he immediately reprimanded himself. "I'll go with you, honey. You're right, sleep can wait."

"No, Carter, you're exhausted." She turned to Sarah. "Besides, this will give us girls a chance to talk without you guys butting in about your sports all the time."

Sarah laughed. "It sounds like fun. Besides, it's too warm for me to sleep, and I need to walk off some of my dinner."

"Come on, Carter. Let the girls take their stroll and I'll

fix us a nightcap before you go to bed," Paul said. He grabbed a flashlight from the glove box and handed it to Sarah. "It gets very dark out here," he explained to Morgan and Carter.

Carter reluctantly walked into the house with his brother. After the babysitter had been paid and sent on her way, Paul joined him in the living room. He didn't sit as Paul had offered, but paced back and forth across the carpeted room. Why was he so damned nervous? He should have insisted on going for a walk with her. He clenched his hands into fists. Why had he let Sheriff Birch put doubts into his mind? Damn him. As hard as he tried, the doubts always seemed to pop back up. His eyes narrowed. Everything would be fine. The women would go for their walk and return in a little while. Nothing would happen. When they returned home he'd personally stop at the sheriff's office and let Jake know that his assumptions were wrong. Even though Jake hadn't bothered him, this would shut him up for good.

"Carter, what's wrong?" Paul asked. "You don't look well."

"I'm fine. Like I said, just a little tired." He sat on the sofa, uneasily sipping the brandy Paul had placed in his hand. A thought suddenly occurred to him. Jake and Mark knew about the trip. He'd told them some time ago. Had they only made him think they'd backed off? Maybe they'd been secretly watching Morgan. How did he know they weren't out there in the shadows right now waiting for the right moment to pounce? He thought about that for a minute. But what would they pounce on? They'd make fools of themselves. Stop, he told himself. Everything is fine. He hoped it was just a short stroll and the women would be back at any moment.

****

"Let's take a walk through the woods behind the house," Morgan said.

"No, it's too dark. Besides, I hate the woods at night," Sarah replied, shivering.

Morgan smiled. "Oh, come on. We won't go too far. Give me the flashlight. We won't go in too far. Come on," she urged.

Sarah hesitated, and then said, "Just not too far in." She handed Morgan the flashlight.

Morgan nodded in agreement. "Have you explored these woods much, Sarah?"

"No, I haven't had the time."

They made small talk as they walked. After several minutes Sarah abruptly stopped.

"What's wrong?" Morgan asked.

"We'd better not go any further," Sarah warned. "We're in too far already."

Morgan took a few more steps, and then turned to her sister-in-law. "Sarah, why don't you like me?" she abruptly asked.

Her question seemed to have caught Sarah off guard. "I like you, Morgan," she said quietly. "Why would you ask that?"

Morgan aimed the beam of light directly at Sarah's face. "Do you?"

Sarah shielded her eyes from the intense glare. "Why do you think that I don't?"

Morgan sighed. "Why is everyone treating me so cruelly?"

"I don't think that's true. None of us know you well. You never speak of anything that gives us an idea of who you really are," she feebly explained. "I'm sorry if you've felt left out. It's just that growing up in Weldon our families were acquainted."

Morgan slipped her hand inside her purse and her fingers closed around the gun. She slowly removed it. "You think I had something to do with the murders, don't you?"

****

Sarah noticed how Morgan's voice had almost become childlike. She swallowed hard. "No, of course I don't, Morgan. I want us to become good friends." Morgan's voice unnerved her.

"I don't believe you. I wish I could, but I can't. You've never wanted to get to know me. I was always the outsider. Everyone wishes Carter would've married a local girl."

"It doesn't matter what anyone else thinks, Morgan. Carter picked you because he fell in love with you. Let's go back now." She started to walk away. Hopefully she could find her way back in the dark.

"Get back here!"

The tone of Morgan's voice startled her. "What?" she whispered hoarsely.

"I'm not ready to go back."

****

Carter finished his drink, and then told Paul he was going to bed. Paul didn't seem worried about the women. He explained that they were probably having a long talk. In fact, he was relieved that they were getting along so well and told Carter he should be, too. An uneasy feeling crept up Carter's spine. Maybe they were lost. He wouldn't sleep until his wife was safely beside him. Paul finished his drink and decided to go to bed, too.

After Carter made sure Paul was inside his own room, he stole back downstairs and sneaked out the back door. He scurried across the large yard until he reached the edge of the woods. This was where he'd seen Sarah and Morgan make their way inside.

CHAPTER SIXTEEN

Morgan aimed the gun at Sarah, laughing to herself because Sarah couldn't see it. She enjoyed her little game, but after a while, she grew tired of it and decided it was time for Sarah to learn the truth. She shone the light on the gun.

Sarah screamed.

"Are you afraid? I just wanted to show you the gun I bought for protection. You don't have to be afraid. I won't let anything happen to you."

"Please put it away," Sarah said.

Morgan laughed. "Let's not play games, Sarah. You know the truth, don't you? You know I killed them. You knew it all along. The funny part is how easy it was to do. And I wouldn't have had a problem if that nosy Mark Barlow hadn't come snooping into my business and convinced the sheriff to keep harassing me."

"Morgan, please. You can get help. I'll help you. Just don't hurt me. Think about Lisa and Terence."

"Do you know how I'm going to explain your death to the authorities? I have it all figured out."

"No, Morgan! I'll do anything. I promise!" she sobbed.

"I'm sorry, Sarah, but I don't accept deals. I've never been a gambler. Besides, you've already betrayed me. You never wanted Carter to marry me, but he did and you won't be happy until he leaves me."

"That's not true. I didn't know you then, but I do now. I know what a sweet person you really are."

"Who the fuck are you kidding?" she snarled. "You treated me like crap!"

Carter stood behind a tree, watching in horror as his beloved wife relayed to Sarah the deaths of his family. Tears poured from his eyes. He shifted and a twig snapped under his foot.

Morgan listened. Probably an animal, she thought. "Look at me, Sarah," she demanded. She aimed the gun and clicked the safety off.

"No!" Carter screamed running toward the women.

Startled by his voice, Morgan turned, giving Sarah the chance to run. She fired a shot in the direction Sarah had taken.

"Carter, go away!" she screamed. "You shouldn't be here."

"No!" Carter cried as he reached her side, and then tried to wrestle the gun from her hand.

She kept her grip on it. "No, Carter, I won't let them take you away from me!" she whimpered.

"Please, put the gun down, honey. I'm not leaving you. You should know that by now," he choked. "I could never leave you."

"No," she whispered. "It's over, isn't it?" A sob caught in her throat. "They took you away from me."

"No, honey. I'm here. I'm not going anywhere." He hadn't noticed that she had changed the position of her arm. He tugged at her arm, hoping she would drop the gun.

The gun discharged. "No!" he screamed. He heard the thud as she hit the ground. He picked up the flashlight that had slipped from her hand. He aimed it at her and saw the blood spurting from her chest. "No," he moaned. "No," he said repeatedly. He knelt beside her, picked up her head, and gently laid it in his lap. He caressed her face as his hot tears splattered on her cheeks.

"Carter," she whispered.

"Don't talk, honey," he sobbed. "Don't talk."

"I love you," she said slowly.

"I love you, too," he cried. "You'll be okay. I promise you."

"No," she whispered. "Take care of Becca." She looked into his eyes. Blood trickled from the corner of her mouth. "I'm scared," she whimpered. "Hold me."

Carter heard sirens in the distance. Sarah must have found her way back to the house and called for help. But he knew it was too late. He lay next to her and gathered her into his arms, shining the light so he could see her beautiful face. Her body went limp, but her eyes still stared at him. He kissed her for the last time, then closed her eyelids, and rested his face on her still warm cheek.

About the Author

Writing is Susan's number one passion. When she isn't writing, she enjoys reading, spending time in her garden, and visiting family and friends. She has many novels, short stories, and magazine articles to her credit. Raised in western New York, she now resides in New Jersey. For information about Susan's current and upcoming titles, please visit http://www.susandroney.com or http://susandroney.blogspot.com

www.ingramcontent.com/pod-product-compliance
Lightning Source LLC
Chambersburg PA
CBHW022016170626
46808CB00001B/444